Ultima Thule Publishing

DALTON DISCOVERY SERIES #1

The Land of the Changing Sun

by

William N. Harben

First Edition: February 2016

Copyright © 2016
Ultima Thule Publishing

ISBN-13: 978-0692625347

Cover Design: *Ethan W. Dempsey*
Interior Formatting: *Ethan W. Dempsey*

Printed in the United States of America

Editor's Note

William Nathaniel Harben was born in Dalton, Georgia on July 5, 1858. From his small town beginnings, Harben developed into one of America's most popular novelists during the first twenty years of the twentieth century. Most well-known for his thirty books and numerous short stories depicting the people of his native north Georgia. *The Land of the Changing Sun* is Harben's only science fiction novel published in 1894. This work is now in the public domain, and out of a desire for Harben's work to reach a new audience I am presenting his work through our Dalton Discovery Series. Dalton has had strong literary ties in its past, and today's readers, I dare say, do not even know of Harben's existence. This will be the first in a series of books bringing back into the limelight public domain works of authors from Dalton, Georgia. It is my hope that today's readers will enjoy these works just as much as the people who were able to read them at the height of their popularity so many years ago.

The text has been updated and modernized to make the reading experience more enjoyable. Spellings have been corrected to reflect today's standards. Hyphens have been eliminated where possible.

-    E.D.

Chapter I

The balloon seemed scarcely to move, though it was slowly sinking toward the ocean of white clouds which hung between it and the earth.

The two inmates of the car were insensible; their faces were bloodless, their cheeks sunken. They were both young and handsome. Harry Johnston, an American, was as dark and sallow as a Spaniard. Charles Thorndyke, an English gentleman, had yellow hair and mustache, blue eyes and a fine intellectual face. Both were tall, athletic in build and well-proportioned.

Johnston was the first to come to consciousness as the balloon sank into less rarefied atmosphere. He opened his eyes dreamily and looked curiously at the white face of his friend in his lap. Then he shook him and tried to call his name, but his lips made no sound. Drawing himself up a little with a hand on the edge of the basket, he reached for a water-jug and sprinkled Thorndyke's face. In a moment he was rewarded by seeing the eyes of the latter slowly open.

"Where are we?" asked Thorndyke in a whisper.

"I don't know;" Johnston answered, "getting nearer to the earth, for we can breathe more easily. I can't remember much after the professor fell from the car. My God, old man! I shall never forget the horror in the poor fellow's eyes as he clung to the rope down there and begged us to save him. I tried to get you to look,

1

but you were dozing off. I attempted to draw him up, but the rope on the edge of the basket was tipping it, and both you and I came near following him. I tried to keep from seeing his horrible face as the rope began to slip through his fingers. I knew the instant he let go by our shooting upward."

"I came to myself and looked over when the basket tipped," replied the Englishman, "I thought I was going too, but I could not stir a muscle to prevent it. He said something desperately, but the wind blew it away and covered his face with his beard, so that I could not see the movement of his lips."

"It may have been some instructions to us about the management of the balloon."

"I think not--perhaps a good-bye, or a message to his wife and child. Poor fellow!"

"How long have we been out of our heads?" and Johnston looked over the side of the car.

"I have not the slightest idea. Days and nights may have passed since he fell."

"That is true. I remember coming to myself for an instant, and it seemed that we were being jerked along at the rate of a gunshot. My God, it was awful! It was as black as condensed midnight. I felt your warm body against me and was glad I was not alone. Then I went off again, but into a sort of nightmare. I thought I was in Hell, and that you were with me, and that Professor Helmholtz was Satan."

"Where can we be?" asked Thorndyke.

"I don't know; I can't tell what is beneath those clouds. It may be earth, sea or ocean; we were evidently whisked along in a storm while we were out of our heads. If we are above the ocean we are lost."

Thorndyke looked over the edge of the car long and attentively, then he exclaimed suddenly:

"I believe it is the ocean."

"What makes you think so?"

"It reflects the sunlight. It is too bright for land. When we got above the clouds at the start it looked darker below than it does now; we may be over the middle of the Atlantic."

"We are going down," said Johnston gloomily.

"That we are, and it means something serious."

Johnston made no answer. Half-an-hour went by. Thorndyke looked at the sun.

"If the professor had not dropped the compass, we could find our bearings," he sighed.

Johnston pointed upward. Thin clouds were floating above them. "We are almost down," he said, and as they looked over the sides of the car they saw the reflection of the sun on the bosom of the ocean, and, a moment later, they caught sight of the blue billows rising and falling.

"I see something that looks like an island," observed Thorndyke, looking in the direction toward which the balloon seemed to be drifting. "It is dark and is surrounded by light. It is far away, but we may reach it if we do not descend too rapidly."

"Throw out the last bag of sand," suggested the American, "we need it as little now as we ever shall."

Thorndyke cut the bag with his knife and watched the sand filter through the bottom of the basket and trail along in a graceful stream behind the balloon. The great flabby bag overhead steadied itself, rose slightly and drifted on toward the dark spot on the vast expanse of sunlit water. They could now clearly see that it was a small island, not more than a mile in circumference.

"How far is it?" asked Thorndyke.

"About two miles," answered the American laconically, "it is a chance for us, but a slim one."

The balloon gradually sank. For twenty minutes the car glided along not more than two hundred feet above the waves. The island was now quite near. It was a barren mound of stone, worn into gullies and sharp precipices

4

by the action of the waves and rain. Hardly a tree or a shrub was in sight.

"It looks like the rocky crown of a great stone mountain hidden in the ocean," said the Englishman; "half a mile to the shore, a hundred feet to the water; at this rate of speed the wind would smash us against those rocks like a couple of bird's eggs dropped from the clouds. We must fall into the water and swim ashore. There is no use trying to save the balloon."

"We had better be about it, then," said Johnston, rising stiffly and holding to the ropes. "If we should go down in the water with the balloon we would get tangled in the ropes and get asphyxiated with the gas. We had better hang down under the basket and let go at exactly the same time."

The water was not more than forty feet beneath, and the island was getting nearer every instant. The two aeronauts swung over on opposite sides of the car and, face to face, hung by their hands beneath.

"I dread the plunge," muttered Thorndyke; "I feel as weak as a sick kitten; I am not sure that I can swim that distance, but the water looks still enough."

"I am played out too," grunted the American, red in the face; "but it looks like our only chance. Ugh! She made a big dip then. We'd better let go. I'll count three, and three is the signal. Now ready. One, two, three!"

Down shot the balloonists and up bounded the great liberated bag of gas; the basket and dangling ropes swung wildly from side to side. The aeronauts touched the water feet foremost at the same instant, and in half a minute they rose, not ten feet apart.

"Now for it," sputtered Johnston, shaking his bushy head like a swimming dog. "Look, the shore is not very far." Thorndyke was saving his wind, and said nothing, but accommodated his stroke to that of his companion, and thus they breasted the gently-rolling billows until finally, completely exhausted, they climbed up the shelving rocks and lay down in the warm sunshine.

"Not a very encouraging outlook," said Johnston, rising when his clothing was dry and climbing a slight elevation. "There is nothing in sight except a waste of stone. Let's go up to that point and look around."

The ascent was exceedingly trying, for the incline was steep and it was at times difficult to get a firm footing. But they were repaid for the exertion, for they had reached the highest point of the island and could see all over it. As far as their vision reached there was nothing beyond the little island except the glistening waves that reached out till they met the sky in all directions. High up in the clouds they saw the balloon, now steadily drifting with the wind toward the south.

"We might as well be dead and done with it," grumbled Thorndyke. "Ships are not apt to approach this isolated spot, and even if they did, how could we give a signal of distress?"

Johnston stroked his dark beard thoughtfully, then he pointed toward the shore.

"There are some driftwood and seaweed," he said; "with my sun-glass I can soon have a bonfire." He took a piece of punk from a waterproof box that he carried in his pocket and focused the sun's rays on it. "Run down and bring me an armful of dry seaweed and wood," he added, intent on his work.

Thorndyke clambered down to the shore, and in a few minutes returned with an armful of fuel. Johnston was blowing his punk into a flame, and in a moment had a blazing fire.

"Good," approved the Englishman, rubbing his hands together over the flames. "We'll keep it burning and it may do some good." Then a smile of satisfaction came over his face as he began to take some clams from his pockets. "Plenty of these fellows down there, and they are as fat and juicy as can be. Hurry up and let's bake them. I'm as hungry as a bear. There is a fine spring of fresh water below, too, so we won't die of thirst."

They baked the clams and ate them heartily, and then went down to the spring near the shore. The water was deliciously cool and invigorating. The sun sank into the quiet ocean and night crept on. The stars came out slowly, and the moon rose full and red from the waves, adding its beams to the flickering light of the fire on the hill-top.

"Suppose we take a walk all round on the beach," proposed the Englishman; "there is no telling what we may find; we may run on something that has drifted ashore from some wrecked ship."

Johnston consented. They had encompassed the entire island, which was oval in shape, and were about to ascend to the rock to put fresh fuel on the fire before lying down to sleep for the night, when Thorndyke noticed a road that had evidently been worn in the rock by human footsteps.

"Made by feet," he said, bending down and looking closely at the rock and raking up a handful of white sand, "but whether the feet of savage or civilized mortal I can't make out."

Johnston was a few yards ahead of him and stooped to pick up something glittering in the moonlight. It was a tap from the heel of a shoe and was of solid silver.

"Civilized," he said, holding it out to his companion; "and of the very highest order of civilization. Whoever heard of people rich enough to wear silver heel-taps?"

"Are you sure it is silver?" asked the Englishman, examining it closely.

"Pure and unalloyed; see how the stone has cut into it, and feel its weight."

"You are right, I believe," returned Thorndyke, as Johnston put the strange trophy into his pocket-book, and the two adventurers paused a moment and looked mutely into each other's eyes.

"We haven't the faintest idea of where we are," said Johnston, his tone showing that he was becoming more despondent. "We don't know how long we were unconscious in the balloon, nor where we were taken in the storm. We may now be in the very center of the North Polar sea--this knob may be the very pivot on which this end of the earth revolves."

The Englishman laughed. "No danger; the sun is too natural. From the poles it would look different."

"I don't mean the old sun that you read so much about, and that they make so much racket over at home, but another of which we are the original discoverer--a sun that isn't in old Sol's beat at all, but one that revolves round the earth from north to south and dips in once a day at the north and the south poles. See?"

The Englishman laughed heartily and slapped his friend on the shoulder.

"I think we are somewhere in the Atlantic; but your finding that heel-tap does puzzle me."

"We are going to have an adventure, beside which all others of our lives will pale into insignificance. I feel it in my bones. See how evenly this road has been worn and it is leading toward the center of the island."

In a few minutes the two adventurers came to a point in the road where tall cliffs on either side stood up perpendicularly. It was dark and cold, and but a faint light from the moon shone down to them.

"I don't like this," said Johnston, who was behind the Englishman; "we may be walking into the ambush of an enemy."

"Pshaw!" and Thorndyke plunged on into the gloomy passage. Presently the walls began to widen like a letter "Y" and in a great open space they saw a placid lake on the bosom of which the moon was shining. On all sides the towering walls rose for hundreds of feet. Speechless with wonder and with quickly-beating hearts they stumbled forward over the uneven road till they reached the shore of the lake. The water was so clear and still that the moon and stars were reflected in it as if in a great mirror.

"Look at that!" exclaimed Thorndyke, pointing down into the depths, "what can that be?"

Johnston followed Thorndyke's finger with his eyes. At first he thought that it was a comet moving across the sky and reflected in the water; but, on glancing above, he saw his mistake. It looked, at first, like a great ball of fire rolling along the bottom of the lake with a stream of flame in its wake.

Chapter II

The two men watched it for several minutes; all the time it seemed to be growing larger and brighter till, after a while, they saw that the light came from something shaped like a ship, sharp at both ends, and covered with oval glass. As it slowly rose to the surface they saw that it contained five or six men, sitting in easy chairs and reclining on luxurious divans. One of them sat at a sort of pilot-wheel and was directing the course of the strange craft, which was moving as gracefully as a great fish.

Then the young men saw the man at the pilot-wheel raise his hand, and from the water came the musical notes of a great bell. The vessel stopped, and one of the men sprang up and raised an instrument that looked like a telescope to his eyes. With this he seemed to be closely searching the lake shores, for he did not move for several minutes. Then he lowered the instrument, and when the bell had rung again, the vessel rose slowly and perpendicularly to the surface and glided to the shore within twenty yards of where the adventurers stood.

"Could they have seen us?" whispered Thorndyke, drawing Johnston nearer the side of the cliff.

"I think so; at all events, they are between us and the outlet; we may as well make the best of it."

The men, all except the pilot, landed, and a dazzling electric search-light was turned on the spot where Thorndyke and Johnston stood. For a moment they were so blinded that they could not see, and then they heard footsteps, and, their eyes becoming accustomed to the light, they found themselves surrounded by several men, very strangely clad. They all wore long cloaks that covered them from head to foot and every man was more than six feet in height and finely proportioned. One of them, who seemed to be an officer in command, bowed politely.

"I am Captain Tradmos, gentlemen, in the king's service. It is my duty to make you my prisoners. I must escort you to the palace of the king."

"That's cool," said Johnston, to conceal the discomfiture that he felt, "We had no idea that you had a kingdom. We have tramped all over this island, and you are the first signs of humanity we have met."

He would have recalled his words before he had finished speaking, if he could have done so, for he saw by the manner of the captain that he had been over bold.

"Follow me," answered the officer curtly, and with a motion of his hand to his men he turned toward the odd-looking vessel.

The two adventurers obeyed, and the cloaked men fell in behind them. Neither Johnston nor Thorndyke had ever seen anything like the peculiar boat that was moored to the rocky shore. It was about forty feet in length, had a hull shaped like a racing yacht, but which was made of black rubber inflated with air. It was covered with glass, save for a doorway about six feet high and three feet wide in the side, and looked like a great oblong bubble floating on the still dark water. As they approached the searchlight was extinguished, and they were enabled to see the boat to a better advantage by the aid of the electric lights that illuminated the interior. It was with feelings of awe that the two adventurers followed the captain across the gang-plank into the vessel.

The electric light was brilliantly white, and in various places pink, red and light-blue screens mellowed it into an artistic effect that was very soothing to the eye. The ceiling was hung with festoons of prisms as brilliant as the purest diamonds, and in them, owing to the gently undulatory movement of the vessel, colors more beautiful than those of a rainbow played entrancingly. Rare pictures in frames of delicate gold were interspersed among the clusters of prisms, and the floor was covered with carpets that felt as soft beneath the foot as pillows of eider-down.

As he entered the door the officer threw off his gray cloak, and his men did likewise, disclosing to view the finest uniforms the prisoners had ever seen. Captain Tradmos's legs were clothed in tights of light-blue silk, and he wore a blue sack-coat of silk plush and a belt of pliant old, the buckles of which were ornamented with brilliant gems. His eyes were dark and penetrating, and his black hair lay in glossy masses on his shoulders. He had the head of an Apollo and a brow indicative of the highest intellect.

Leaving his men in the first room that they entered, he gracefully conducted his prisoners through another room to a small cabin in the stern of the boat, and told them to make themselves comfortable on the luxurious couches that lined the circular glass walls.

"Our journey will be of considerable length," he said, "and as you are no doubt fatigued, you had better take all the rest you can get. I see that you need food and have ordered a repast which will refresh you." As he concluded he touched a button in the wall and instantly a table, laden with substantial food, rare delicacies and wines, rose through a trap-door in the floor. He smiled at the expressions of surprise on their faces and touched a green bottle of wine with his white tapering hand.

"The greater part of our journey will be under water, and our wines are specially prepared to render us capable of subsisting on a rather limited quantity of air during the voyage, so I advise you to partake of them freely; you will find them very agreeable to the taste."

"We are very grateful," bowed Thorndyke, from his seat on a couch. "I am sure no prisoners were ever more graciously or royally entertained. To be your prisoner is a pleasure to be remembered."

"Till our heads are cut off, anyway," put in the irrepressible American.

Tradmos smiled good-humoredly.

"I shall leave you now," he said, and with a bow he withdrew.

"This is an adventure in earnest," whispered Johnston; "My stars! What can they intend to do with us?"

"One of the first things will be to take us down to the bottom of this lake where we saw them a while ago, and I don't fancy it at all; what if this blasted glass-case should burst? We may have dropped into a den of outlaws on a gigantic scale, and it may be necessary to put us out of the way to keep our mouths closed."

"I am hungry, and am going to eat," said the American, drawing a cushioned stool up to the table. "Here goes for some of the wine; remember, it is a sort of breath-restorer. I am curious enough not to want to collapse till I have seen this thing through. He said something about a palace and a king. Where can we be going?"

"Down into the center of the earth, possibly," and the handsome Englishman moved a stool to the table and took the glass of green-colored wine that Johnston pushed toward him. "Some scientists hold that the earth is filled with water instead of fire. Who knows where this blamed thing may not take us? Here is to a safe return from the amphibious land!"

Both drank their wine simultaneously, lowered their glasses at the same instant, and gazed into each other's eyes.

"Did you ever taste such liquor?" asked Thorndyke, "it seems to run like streams of fire through every vein I have."

Johnston shook his head mutely, and held the sparkling effervescing fluid between him and the light.

"Ugh! Take it down," cried the Englishman, "it throws a green color on your face that makes you look like a corpse." Johnston clinked the glass against that of his companion and they drained the glasses. "Hush, what was that?" asked Thorndyke.

There was a sound like boiling water outside and as if air were being pumped out of some receptacle, and the vessel began to move up and down in a lithe sort of fashion and to bend tortuously from side to side like a great sluggish fish. Through the partitions of glass they saw one of the men closing the door, and in a moment the vessel glided away from the shore. The men all sank into easy positions on the couches, and delightful music as soft as an Aeolian lyre seemed to be breathed from the walls and floor. Then the music seemed to die away and a bell down in the vessel's hull rang.

"We are in the middle of the lake," said Thorndyke, looking through the glass toward the black cliffy shore; "the next thing will be our descent. I wonder----"

But he was unable to proceed, and Johnston noticed in alarm that his eyes were slightly protruding from their sockets. The air seemed suddenly to become more compact as if compressed, and the water was set into such violent commotion that it was dashed against the glass sides in billows as white as snow. Then Johnston found that he could not breathe freely, and he understood the trouble of the Englishman.

Captain Tradmos came suddenly to the door. He was smiling as he motioned toward the wines on the table.

"You had better drink more of the wine," he advised sententiously.

Both of the captives rushed to the table. The instant they had swallowed the wine they felt relieved, but were still weak. The captain bowed and went away. Thorndyke's hand trembled as he refilled his friend's glass. "I thought I was gone up," he said, "I never had such a choky sensation in my life; you are still purple in the face."

"Eat of what is before you," said the captain, looking in at the door; "you cannot stand the increasing pressure unless you do."

They needed no second invitation, for they were half-famished. The fish and meat were delicious, and the bread was delightfully sweet.

"Look outside!" cried Johnston. The water was now still, but it was gradually rising up the sides of the boat, and in a moment it had closed over the crystal roof. Both of the captives were conscious of a heavy sensation in the head and a dull roaring in the ears. Down they went, at first slowly and then more rapidly, till it seemed to them that they had descended over a thousand feet. Great monsters like whales swam to the vessel, as if attracted by the lights, and their massive bodies jarred against the glass walls as they turned to swim away. They sank about five hundred feet lower; and all at once the lights went out, and the boat gradually stopped.

It was at once so dark that the two captives could not see each other, though only the width of the table separated them. Everything was profoundly still; not a sound came from the men in the other rooms. Presently Thorndyke whispered, "Look, do you see that red light overhead?"

"Yes," said Johnston, "it looks like a star."

"It is our bonfire," said Thorndyke, "that's what betrayed us."

Again the vessel began to sink, and more rapidly than ever; indeed, as Thorndyke expressed it, he had the cool feeling that nervous people experience in going down quickly in an elevator.

"If we go any lower," he added, as the great rubber hull seemed to struggle like some living monster, "the sides of this thing will collapse like an egg-shell and we will be as flat as pancakes."

"You need not fear, we have much lower to go!" It was the captain's voice, but they could not tell from whence it came. Then they heard again the seductive music, and it was so soothing that they soon fell asleep.

18

They had no idea how long they had slept, but they were awakened by the ringing of a bell and felt the vessel was coming to a stop. They were still far beneath the surface; indeed, the boat was resting on the bottom, for in the light of two or three powerful search-lights they saw a wide succession of submerged hills, vales, and rugged cliffs. Before them was a great mountainside and in it they saw the mouth of a dark tunnel. They had scarcely noticed it before the vessel rose a little and glided toward the tunnel and entered it. Through the glass walls they could see that it was narrow, and that the ragged sides and roof were barely far enough apart to admit them.

Suddenly one of the men came in and drew a curtain down behind them, and, with a vexed look on his face retired.

When he was gone Johnston put his lips close to Thorndyke's ear and whispered:

"Did you see that?"

"See what?"

"Just as he drew the curtain down I saw what looked to me like a cliff of solid gold. It had been dug out into a cavern in which I saw a vessel like this, and men in diving suits digging and loading it."

This took the Englishman's breath away for a moment, then he remarked: "That accounts for the heel-tap we found; who knows, these people may be possessors of the richest gold and silver mines on earth."

The bell rang again. "We are rising," said Johnston. "If this is the only way of reaching the king's domain, we could never get back to civilization unless they release us of their own accord, that's certain!"

"Heavens, isn't it still!" exclaimed the Englishman. "The machinery of this thing moves as noiselessly as the backbone of an eel. I wish I could understand its works."

"I am more concerned about where we are going. I tell you we are being taken to some wonderful place. People who can construct such marvels of mechanical skill as this boat will not be behind in other things; then look at the physiques of those giants."

Just then the man who had drawn down the shade came in and raised it. Both the captives pretended to be uninterested in his movements, but when he had withdrawn they looked through the glass eagerly.

"See," whispered Thorndyke, in the ear of his companion, "the walls are close to us, and are as perpendicular as those of the lake in which they found us."

Johnston said nothing. His attention was riveted to the walls of rock; the vessel was rising rapidly. An hour passed. The soft music had ceased, and the air seemed less dense and fresher. Then the waters suddenly parted over the roof and ran in crystal streams down the oval glass.

They were on the surface, and the vessel was slowly gliding toward the shore which could not be seen owing to there now being no light except that inside the boat. Captain Tradmos entered, followed by two of his men holding black silken bandages.

"We must blindfold you," he said; "captives are not allowed to see the entrance to our kingdom."

Without a word they submitted.

"This way," said the captain kindly, and, holding to an arm of each, he piloted them out of the vessel to the shore. Then he led them through what they imagined to be a long stone corridor or arcade from the ringing echoes of their feet on the stone pavement. Presently they came to what seemed to be an elevator, for when they had entered it and sat down, they heard a metallic door slide back into its place, and they descended quickly.

They could form no idea as to the distance they went down; but Thorndyke declared afterward that it was over ten thousand feet. When the elevator stopped Captain Tradmos led them out, and both of the captives were conscious of breathing the purest, most invigorating air they had ever inhaled. Instantly their strength returned, and they felt remarkably buoyant as they were led along over another pavement of polished stone.

21

Tradmos laughed. "You like the atmosphere?"

"I never heard of anything like it," said Thorndyke. "It is so delightful I can almost taste it."

"It was that which made Alpha what it is--the most wonderful country in the universe," said the officer. "There is much in store for you."

The ears of the two captives were greeted by a vague, indefinable hum, like and yet unlike that of a busy city. It was like many far-off sounds carefully muffled. Now and then they heard human voices, laughter, and singing in the distance, and the twanging of musical instruments.

Then they knew that they were entering a building of some sort, for they heard a key turn in a lock and the humming sound in the distance was cut off. They felt a soft carpet under their feet, and the feet of their guards no longer clinked on the stones.

When the bandages were removed they found themselves in a sumptuous chamber, alone with the captain. The brilliant light from a quaintly-shaped candelabrum, in the center of the chamber, dazzled them, but in a few minutes their eyes had become accustomed to it.

Tradmos seemed to be enjoying the looks of astonishment on their faces as they glanced at the different objects in the room.

"It is night," he said smilingly. "You need rest after your voyage. Lie down on the beds and sleep. Tomorrow you will be conducted to the palace of the king."

With a bow he withdrew, and they heard a massive bolt slide into the socket of a door hidden behind a curtain. The two men gazed at each other without speaking, for a moment, and then they began to inspect the room.

In alcoves half-veiled with silken curtains stood statues in gold and bronze. The walls and ceilings were decorated with pictures unlike any they had ever seen. Before one, the picture of an angel flying through a dark, star-filled sky, they both stood enchanted.

"What is it?" asked Thorndyke, finding voice finally. "It is not done with brush or pencil; the features seem alive and, by Jove, you can actually see it breathe. Don't you see the clouds gliding by, and the wings moving?"

"It is light--it is formed by light!" declared the other enthusiastically, and he ran to the wall, about six feet from the picture, and put his hand on a square metal box screwed to the wall.

"I have it," he said quickly, "come here!"

The Englishman advanced curiously and examined the box.

"Don't you see that tiny speck of light in the side towards the picture? Well, the view is thrown from this box on the wall, and it is the motion of the powerful light that gives apparent life to the angel. It is wonderful."

In a commodious alcove, in a glow of pink light from above, was a life-sized group of musicians--statues in colored metal of a Spanish girl playing a manor, an Italian with a slender calascione, a Russian playing his jorbon, and an African playing a banjo. Luxurious couches hung by spiral springs from the ceiling to a convenient height from the floor, and here and there lay rugs of rare beauty and great ottomans of artistic designs and colors.

"We ought to go to bed," proposed Thorndyke; "we shall have plenty of time to see this Aladdin's land before we get away from it."

There were two large downy beds on quaintly wrought bedsteads of brass, but the two captives decided to sleep together.

Thorndyke was the first to awaken. The lights in the candelabrum were out, but a gray light came in at the top and bottom of the window. He rose and drew the heavy curtain of one of the windows aside. He shrank back in astonishment.

Chapter III

"What is it, Thorndyke? What are you looking at?" And the American slowly left the bed and approached his friend.

Thorndyke only held the curtain further back and watched Johnston's face as he looked through the wide plate-glass window.

"My gracious!" ejaculated the latter as he drew nearer. It was a wondrous scene. The building in which they were imprisoned stood on a gentle hill clad in luxuriant, smoothly-cut grass and ornamented with beautiful flowers and plants; and below lay a splendid city--a city built on undulating ground with innumerable grand structures of white marble, with turrets, domes and pinnacles of gold. Wide streets paved in polished stone and bordered with lush-green grass interspersed with statues and beds and mounds of strange plants and flowers stretched away in front of them till they were lost in the dim, misty distance. Parks filled with pavilions, pleasure-lakes, fountains, and tortuous drives and walks, dotted the landscape in all directions.

Thorndyke's breath had clouded the glass of the window, and he rubbed it with his handkerchief. As he did so the sash slowly, and without a particle of sound, slid to one side, disclosing a narrow balcony outside. It had a graceful balustrade, made of carved red-and-white mottled marble, and on the end of the balcony facing the city sat a great gold and silver jug, ten feet high, of rare design. The spout was formed by the body of a dragon with wings extended; the handle was a serpent with the extremity of its tail coiled around the neck of the jug.

The air that came in at the window was fresh and dewy, and laden with the most entrancing odors. Thorndyke led the way out, treading very gently at first. Johnston followed him, too much surprised to make any comment. From this position, their view to the left round the corner of the building was widened, and new wonders appeared on every hand.

Over the polished stone pavements strange vehicles ran noiselessly, as if the wheels had cushioned tires, and the streets were crowded with an active, strangely-clad populace.

"Look at that!" exclaimed the American, and from a street corner they saw a queer-looking machine, carrying half-a-dozen passengers, rise like a bird with wings outspread and fly away toward the east. They watched it till it disappeared in the distance.

"We are indeed in wonderland," said the Englishman; "I can't make head nor tail of it. We were on an isolated island, the Lord only knows where, and have suddenly been transported to a new world!"

"I can't feel at all as if we were in the world we were born in," returned Johnston. "I feel strange."

"The wine," suggested the Englishman, "you know it did wonders for us in that subwater thing."

"No; the wine has nothing to do with it. My head never was clearer. The very atmosphere is peculiar. The air is invigorating, and I can't get enough of it."

"That is exactly the way I feel," was Thorndyke's answer.

"Look at the sunlight," went on Johnston; "it is gray like our dawn, but see how transparent it is. You can look through it for miles and miles. It is becoming pink in the east, the sun will soon be up, and I am curious to see it."

"It must be up now, but we cannot see it for the hills and buildings. My goodness, see that!" and the Englishman pointed to the east. A flood of delicate pink light was now pouring into the vast body of gray and was slowly driving the more somber color toward the west. The line of separation was marked--so marked, indeed, that it seemed a vast, rose-colored billow rolling, widening and sweeping onward like a swell of the ocean shoreward. On it came rapidly, till the whole landscape was magically changed. The flowers, the trees, the grass, the waters of the lakes, the white buildings, the costumes of the people in the streets, even the sky, changed in aspect. The white clouds looked like fire-lit smoke, and far toward the west rolled the long line of pink still struggling with the gray and driving it back.

The sun now came into sight, a great bleeding ball of fire slowly rising above the gilded roofs in the distance.

"By Jove, look at our shadows!" exclaimed Johnston, and both men gazed at the balcony floor in amazement; their shadows were as clearly defined and black as silhouettes. "How do you account for that?" continued the American, "I am firmly convinced that this sun is not the orb that shines over my native land."

Thorndyke laughed, but his laugh was forced. "How absurd! And yet--" He extended his hand over the balustrade into the rosy glow, and without concluding his remark held it back into the shadow of the window-casement. "By Jove!" he exclaimed; "there is not a particle of warmth in it. It is exactly the same temperature in the shade as in the light." He moved back against the wall. "No; there is no difference; the blamed thing doesn't give out any warmth."

Johnston's hands were extended in the light. "I believe you are right," he declared in awe, "something is wrong."

At that moment appeared from the room behind them a handsome youth, attired in a suit of scarlet silk that fitted his athletic figure perfectly. He rapped softly on the window-casement and bowed when they turned.

"Your breakfast is waiting for you," he announced. They followed him into a room adjoining the one they had occupied, and found a table holding a sumptuous repast. The boy gave them seats and handed them golden plates to eat upon. The fruits, wine and meats were very appetizing, and they ate with relish.

"I believe we are to be conducted to the palace of your king tomorrow," ventured the Englishman to the boy.

The boy shook his head, but made no reply, and busied himself with removing the dishes. As they were rising from the table, they heard footsteps in the hall outside. The door opened. It was Captain Tradmos, and he was accompanied by a tall, bearded man with a leather case under his arm.

"You must undergo a medical examination," the captain said smilingly. "It is our invariable custom, but this is by a special order from the king."

Johnston shuddered as he looked at the odd-looking instruments the medical man was taking from the case, but Thorndyke watched his movements with phlegmatic indifference. He stood erect; threw back his shoulders; expanded his massive chest and struck it with his clenched fist in pantomimic boastfulness.

Tradmos smiled genially; but there was something curt and official in his tone when he next spoke that took the Englishman slightly aback. "You must bare your breast over your heart and lungs," he said; and while Thorndyke was unbuttoning his shirt, he and the medical man went to the door and brought into the room a great golden bell hanging in a metallic frame.

The bell was so thin and sensitive to the slightest jar or movement that, although it had been handled with extreme care, the captives could see that it was vibrating considerably, and the room was filled with a low metallic sound that not only affected the ear of the hearer but set every nerve to tingling. The medical man stopped the sound by laying his hand upon the bell. To a tube in the top of the bell he fastened one end of a rubber pipe; the other end was finished with a silver device shaped like the mouth-piece of a speaking tube. This he firmly pressed over the Englishman's heart. Thorndyke winced and bit his lip, for the strange thing took hold of his flesh with the tenacity of a powerful suction-pump.

"Ouch!" he exclaimed playfully, but Johnston saw that he had turned pale, and that his face was drawn as if from pain.

"Hold still!" ordered the medical man; "it will be over in a minute; now, be perfectly quiet and listen to the bell!"

The Englishman stood motionless, the sinews of his neck drawn and knotted, his eyes starting from their sockets. Thorndyke felt the rubber tube quiver suddenly and writhe with the slow energy of a dying snake, and then from the quivering bell came a low, gurgling sound like a stream of water being forced backward and forward.

Tradmos and the medical man stepped to the bell and inspected a small dial on its top.

"What was that?" gasped the Englishman, purple in the face.

"The sound of your blood," answered Tradmos, as he removed the instrument from Thorndyke's flesh; "it is as regular as mine; you are very lucky; you are slightly fatigued, but you will be sound in a day or two."

"Thank you," replied the Englishman, but he sank into a chair, overcome with weakness.

"Now, I'll take you, please," said the medical man, motioning Johnston to rise.

"I am slightly nervous," apologized the latter, as he stood up and awkwardly fumbled the buttons of his coat.

"Nervousness is a mental disease," said the man, with professional brusqueness; "it has nothing to do with the body except to dominate it at times. If you pass your examination you may live to overcome it."

The American looked furtively at Thorndyke, but the head of the Englishman had sunk on his breast and he seemed to be asleep. Johnston had never felt so lonely and forsaken in his life. From his childhood he had entertained a secret fear that he had inherited heart disease, and like Maupassant's "Coward," who committed suicide rather than meet a man in a duel, he had tried in vain to get away from the horrible, ever-present thought by plunging into perilous adventures.

31

At that moment he felt that he would rather die than know the worst from the uncanny instrument that had just tortured his strong comrade till he was overcome with exhaustion.

"I never felt better in my life," he said falteringly, but it seemed to him that every nerve and muscle in his frame was withering through fear.
His tongue felt clumsy and thick and his knees were quivering as with ague.

"Stand still," ordered the physician sternly, and Johnston was further humiliated by having Tradmos sympathetically catch hold of his arm to steady him.

"Your people are far advanced in the sciences," went on the physician coldly, "but there are only a few out of their number who know that the mind governs the body and that fear is its prime enemy. Five minutes ago you were eating heartily and had your share of physical strength, and yet the mere thought that you are now to know the actual condition of your most vital organ has made you as weak as an infant. If you kept up this state of mind for a month it would kill you.

"Now listen," he went on, as the instrument gripped Johnston's flesh and the rubber tube began to twist and move as if charged with electricity. The American held his breath. A sound as of water being forced through channels that were choked, mingled with a wheezing sound like wind escaping from a broken bellows came from the bell.

"Your frame is all right," said the medical man, as he released the trembling American, "but you have long believed in the weakness of your heart and it has, on that account, become so. You must banish all fear from your thoughts. You perhaps know that we have a place specially prepared for those who are not physically sound. I am sorry that you do not stand a better examination."

Tradmos regarded the American with a look of sympathy as he gave him a chair and then rang a bell on the table. Thorndyke looked up sleepily, as an attendant entered with a couple of parcels, and glanced wonderingly at his friend's white face and bloodshot eyes.

"What's the matter?" he asked; but Johnston made no reply, for the captain had opened the parcels and taken out two suits of silken clothing.

"Put them on," he said, giving a suit of gray to Johnston and one of light blue to Thorndyke. "We shall leave you to change your attire, and I shall soon come for you."

Chapter IV

In a few minutes the captain returned and found his prisoners ready to go with him. Thorndyke looked exceedingly handsome in his glossy tights, close-fitting sack-coat, tinsel belt and low shoes with buckles of gold. The natural color had come back into his cheeks, and he was exhilarated over the prospect of further adventure.

It was not so, however, with poor Johnston; his spirits had been so dampened by the physician's words that he could not rally from his despondency. His suit fitted his figure as well as that of the Englishman, but he could not wear it with the same hopeful grace.

"Cheer up!" whispered Thorndyke, as they followed the captain through a long corridor, "if we are on our way to the stake or block we are at least going dressed like gentlemen."

Outside they found the streets lined with spectators eagerly waiting to see them pass. The men all had suits like those which had been given the captives, and the women wore flowing gowns like those of ancient Greece.

"These are the common people," whispered Thorndyke to Johnston, "but did you ever dream of such perfect features and physiques? Every face is full of merriment and good cheer. I am curious to see the royalty."

Johnston made no reply, for Captain Tradmos turned suddenly and faced them.

"Stand here till I return," he said, and he went back into the house.

"Where in the deuce do you think we are?" pursued Thorndyke with a grim smile.

"Haven't the slightest idea," sighed Johnston, and he shuddered as he looked down the long white street with its borders of human faces.

Thorndyke was observant.

"There is not a breath of air stirring," he said; "and yet the atmosphere is like impalpable delicacies to a hungry man's stomach. Look at that big tree, not a leaf is moving, and yet every breath I draw is as fresh as if it came from a mountain-top. Did you ever see such flowers as those? Look at that ocean of orchids."

"They think we are a regular monkey-show," grumbled the American. "Look how the crowd is gaping and shoving and fighting for places to see us."

"It's your legs they want to behold, old fellow. Do you know I never knew you had such knotty knee-joints; did you ever have rheumatism? I wish I had 'em; they wouldn't put me to death--they would make me the chief attraction in the royal museum." Thorndyke concluded his jest with a laugh, but the face of his friend did not brighten.

"You bet that medical examination meant something serious," he said.

"Pooh!" and the Englishman slapped his friend playfully on the shoulder.

"Since I have seen that vast crowd of well-developed people, and remember what that medicine man said, I have made up my mind that we are going to be separated." Poor Johnston's lip was quivering.

"Rubbish! but there comes the captain; put on a bold front; talk up New York; tell 'em about Chicago and the Fair, and ask to be allowed to ride in their Ferris Wheel--if they ain't got no wheel, ask 'em when the first train leaves town."

"This is no time for jokes," growled Johnston, as Tradmos returned. Tradmos motioned to something that in the distance looked like a carriage, but which turned out to be a flying machine. It rose gracefully and glided over the ground and settled at their feet. It was large enough to seat a dozen people, and there was a little glass-windowed compartment at the end in which they could see "the driver," as he was termed by Tradmos. The mysterious machinery was hidden in the woodwork overhead and beneath.

"Get in," said the captain, and the door flew open as if of its own accord. Thorndyke went in first and was followed by the moody American. "Let up on the ague," jested Thorndyke, nudging his friend with his elbow; "if you keep on quivering like that you may shake the thing loose from its moorings and we'd never know what became of us."

Johnston scowled, and the officer, who had overheard the remark, smiled as he leaned toward the window and gave some directions to the man in the other compartment.

"You both take it rather coolly," he remarked to Thorndyke. "I took a man and a woman over this route several years ago and both of them were in a dead faint; but, in fact, you have nothing to fear. We never have accidents."

"It is as safe as a balloon, I suppose, and we are at home in them," said the Englishman, with just the hint of a swagger in his tone.

"But your balloons are poor, primitive things at best," returned Tradmos in his soft voice. "They can't be compared to this mode of travel, though, of course, our machines would not operate in your atmosphere."

"Why not?" impulsively asked the Englishman. "I thought----"

But he did not conclude his remark, for they were rising, and both he and Johnston leaned apprehensively forward and looked out of one of the windows. Down below the long lines of people were silently waving their hats, scarfs and handkerchiefs as the machine swept along over their heads. As they rose higher the scene below widened like a great circular fan, and in the delicate roselight, the whole so appealed to Thorndyke's artistic sense that he exclaimed:

"Glorious! Superb! Transcendent!" and he directed Johnston's attention to the wonderful pinkish haze which lay over the view toward the west like a vast diaphanous web of rosy sunbeams.

"You ask why our air-ships would not operate in your atmosphere," said the captain, showing pleasure at Thorndyke's enthusiasm. "It is simple enough when you have studied the climatic differences between the two countries. You have much to contend with--the winds, for instance, the heat and cold, etc.; this is the only known country where the winds are subjugated. I have never been in your world, but from what I have heard of it I am not anxious to see it. Your atmosphere and climate are so changeable and so diverse in different localities that I have heard your people spend much of their time in seeking congenial climes. I think it was a man who came from London that claimed he once had a cold--'a bad cold,' I think he called it. It was a standing joke in the royal family for a long time, and he heard so much about it that he tried to deny what he had said!"

Johnston glanced at the speaker non-plussed, but the captain was looking at Thorndyke.

"Your climate is delightful here now," said the Englishman; "is it so long at a time?"

"Perpetually; it is regulated every moment, and every year we perfect it in some way."

"Perfect it?"

"Yes, of course, why not? If it ever fails to be up to the usual high standard, it is owing to neglect of those in charge, and neglect is punished severely."

Thorndyke's eyes sought those of the American incredulously. Seeing which Tradmos looked amused.

"You doubt it," he smiled. "Well, wait till you have been here longer. The fact is, any one born in our climate could not live in yours. The king experimented on a man who claimed to have only one lung, but who had two sound ones when he was cut open. Well, the king sent him to China, or America, or some such place, and he wheezed himself to death in a week by your clocks. The weather was too fickle for him. Our system has been perfected to such an extent that we live four lives to your one, and our fruits and vegetables are a hundred percent. better than those in other countries."

"What is the name of your country?" asked Thorndyke, feeling that he was not losing anything by his boldness.

"Alpha."

"Where is it located?"

"I don't know." Tradmos looked out at the window for a moment as if to ascertain that they were going in the right direction, then he fixed his dark eyes on Thorndyke and asked hesitatingly:--

"I never thought--I--but do you know where your country is located?"

"Why, certainly."

"Well, I don't know where this one is. We are taught everything, I think, except geography." Nothing more was said for several minutes, then an exclamation of admiration broke from the Englishman. The color of the sunlight was changing. From east to west within the entire arc of their observation rolled an endless billow of lavender light leaving a placid sea of the same color behind it. On it swept, slowly driving back the pink glow that had been over everything.

"I see you like our sunlight?" said Tradmos, half interrogatively.

"Never saw anything like it before."

"Yours is, I think, the same color all day long."

"Except on rainy days."

"Must be a great bore, monotonous--too much sameness. It is white, is it not?"

"Yes, rather--between white and yellow, I call it."

"Something like our sixth hour, I suppose; this is the fourth hour of morning. Then come blue, yellow, green, and at noon red. The afternoon is divided up in the same way. The first hour is green, then follow yellow, blue, lavender, rose, gray and purple. Yes, I should think you would find yours somewhat tiresome."

"We can rely on it," said Johnston speaking for the first time and in a wavering voice, "it is always there."

"Doing business at the old stand," laughed Thorndyke, attempting an Americanism.

"Well, that is a comfort, anyway," said the captain seriously. "In my time they have had no solar trouble, but some of the old people tell horrible tales of a period when our sun for several days did not shine at all."

"Can it be possible?" said the Englishman dubiously.

"Oh, yes; and the early settlers had a great deal of trouble in different ways; but I am not at liberty to give you information on that head. It is the king's special pleasure to have newcomers form their own impressions, and he is particularly fond of noting their surprise, and, above all, their approval. People usually come here of their own accord through the influence of our secret force of agents all over the earth, but you were brought because you happened to drop on our island and would have found out too much for our good, and that red light you kept burning night and day might have given us trouble. There is no telling how long you could have kept alive on those clams."

"We meant no offence," apologized Thorndyke; "we----"

"Oh, I know it, I was only explaining the situation," interrupted the officer.

"What is that bright spot to the right?" asked Thorndyke, to change the subject.

"The king's palace; that is the dome. We shall soon be there. Now, I must not talk to you any longer. Somebody may be watching us with glasses. I have taken a liking to you, and some time, when I get the opportunity, I shall give you some useful advice, but I must treat you very formally, at least till you have had audience with the king."

"Thank you," said the Englishman, and Tradmos stood up in the car to watch their progress through the circular glass of a little cupola on top. Thorndyke smiled at Johnston, but the American was in no pleasant mood. The indifference with which Tradmos had treated him had nettled him.

The machine was now slowly descending. A vast pile of white marble, with many golden domes and spires, rose between them and the earth below.

"To the balcony on the central dome," ordered Tradmos through the window of the driver's compartment; and the adventurers felt the car sweep round in a curve that threw them against each other, and the next moment they had landed on a wide iron balcony encircling a great golden cone that towered hundreds of feet above them.

Chapter V

"Follow me," said the captain stiffly, for there were several guards in white and gold uniforms pacing to and fro on the battlement-like walls. He led the two adventurers through a door in the base of the dome. At first they were dazed by a brilliant light from above, and looking up they beheld a marvel of kaleidoscopic colors formed by a myriad of electric-lighted prisms sloping gradually from the floor to the apex of the dome. Thorndyke could compare it to nothing but a stupendous diamond, the very heart of which the eye penetrated.

"Don't look at it now," advised Tradmos, in an undertone; "it was constructed to be seen from below, and to light the great rotunda."

Mutely the captives obeyed. At every turn they were greeted with a new wonder. The captain now led them round a narrow balcony on the inside of the vast dome, and, looking over the railing down below, they saw a vast tessellated pavement made of polished stones of various and brilliant colors and so artistically arranged that, from where they stood, lifelike pictures of landscapes seemed to rise to meet the vision wherever the eye rested. Statues of white marble, gold and bronze were placed here and there, and, in squares of living green, fountains threw up streams of crystal water. Tradmos paused for them to look down and smiled at their evident admiration.

"How far is it down there?" Thorndyke ventured to ask.

"Over a thousand feet," replied Tradmos. "Look across opposite and you will see that there are fifty floors beneath us, and each floor has a balcony like this overlooking the court."

"What is the sound that comes up from below?" asked the Englishman.

"It is the voices of the people and their footsteps on the stone."

"What people?"

"Don't you see them? Your eyes are dazzled by the light; I ought to have warned you against looking up into the dome. The people are down there; do the views in the pavement not look a little blurred?"

"Yes."

"Well, if you will look more closely you will see that it is a multitude of people."

"Great heavens!" exclaimed the Englishman, and he became deeply absorbed in the contemplation of the rarest sight he had ever seen. As he looked closely he noticed a black spot growing larger and nearer, and he glanced inquiringly at the captain.

"It is an elevator. There are a great many of them used in the palace, but none have happened to rise as high as

this since we came. The one you see is coming for us."
The next moment the strange vehicle was floating
toward them. The captain opened the door and
preceded the captives into the interior.

"The royal audience chamber," he said, carelessly, to the
driver behind the glass of the adjoining compartment,
and down they floated as lightly as a bubble--down past
balcony after balcony, laden with moving throngs, until
they alighted in a great conservatory.

Near them was a tall fountain the water of which was
playing weird music on great bells of glass, some of
which hung in the fountain's stream and others rose and
fell, giving forth strange, submerged tones in the
foaming basin.

"It is a new invention recently placed here by the king's
son who is a musical genius," explained Tradmos. "You
will be astonished at some of his inventions."

He led them, as if to avoid the great crowds that they
could now hear on all sides, down a long vista of palms,
the branches of which met over their heads, to the wide
door of the audience chamber. A party of men dressed
in uniforms of white silk with gold and silver ornaments
bowed before the captain and made way for him.

The captives now found themselves in the most
splendid and spacious room they had ever seen, at the
far end of which was a long dais and on it an elaborate
throne.

"I shall be obliged to leave you when the king comes," said Tradmos to Thorndyke, "but I shall hope to see you again. Don't forget my name and rank, for I may send you a message some time that may aid you." "Thank you," replied the Englishman, and then as a throng of beautiful young women came from a room on the side and gathered about the throne he added inquisitively: "Who are they?"

"The wives and daughters of the king and the wives of the princes," was the cautious answer, "but don't look at any one of them closely."

"I don't see how a fellow can help it; they are ravishingly beautiful, don't you think so, Johnston?"

"Don't be a fool," snapped the American, "don't you know enough to hold your tongue."

Tradmos smiled as if amused, and when he had shown them to seats near the great golden throne, he said:

"Stay where you are till the king sends for you, and then go and kneel before the throne. Do not rise till he bids you."

The captives thanked him and the captain turned away. The eyes of all the royal party now rested on the strangers, and it was hard for them to appear unconscious of it. A great crowd was slowly filling the room and an orchestra in a balcony on the left of the dais began to make delightful music on instruments the

46

strangers had never before seen. After an entrancing prelude a sound of singing was heard, and far up in a grand dome, lighted like the one the captives had just admired over the central court of the palace, they saw a bevy of maidens, robed in white, moving about in mid-air, apparently unsupported by anything.

"How on earth is that done?" asked Thorndyke.

"I don't know," returned Johnston, speaking more freely now that the captain had gone. "I am not surprised at anything."

"Their voices are exquisite, and that orchestra--a Boston symphony concert couldn't be compared to it."

"There goes the sunlight again," cried Johnston, "by Jove, it is blue!"

The transition was sublime. They seemed transported to some other scene. The great multitude, the elegantly-dressed attendants about the throne, the courtiers, the beautiful women, all seemed to change in appearance; on the view through the wide doors leading to the conservatory, and the great swarming court beyond, the soft blue light fell like a filmy veil of enchantment.

"Wonderful!" exclaimed the American.

"It is ahead of our clocks, anyway," jested Thorndyke. "Any child that can count on its fingers could tell that this is the fifth hour of the day."

The music grew louder; there was a harmonious blare of mighty trumpets, the clang of gongs and cymbals, and then the music softened till it could scarcely be heard. There was commotion about the throne.

The king was coming. Every person on the dais stood motionless, expectant. A page drew aside the rich curtain from a door on the right, and an old man, wearing a robe of scarlet ornamented with jewels and a crown set with sparkling gems, entered and seated himself on the throne. The music sank lower; so soft did it become that the tinkling bells of the great fountain outside could be heard throughout the room.

The king bowed to the throng on the dais and spoke a few words to a courtier who advanced as he sat down. The courtier must have spoken of them, for the king at once looked down at Johnston and Thorn-dyke and nodded his head. The courtier spoke to a page, and the youth left the dais and came toward the captives.

"We are in for it," cautioned Thorndyke, "now don't be afraid of your shadow; we'll come out all right."

"The king has sent for you," said the page, the next instant. "Go to the throne."

They were the cynosure of the entire room as they went up the carpeted steps of the dais and knelt before the king.

Chapter VI

"Rise!" commanded the king, in a deep, well-modulated voice, and when they had arisen he inspected them critically, his eyes lingering on Thorndyke.

"You look as if you take life easily; you have a jovial countenance," he said cordially.

Thorndyke returned his smile and at once felt at ease.

"There is no use in taking it any other way," he said; "it doesn't amount to much at best."

"You are wrong," returned the king, playing with the jewels on his robe, "that is because you have been reared as you have--in your unsystematic world. Here we make life a serious study. It is our object to assist nature in all things. The efforts of your people amount to nothing because they are not carried far enough. Your scientists are dreaming idiots. They are continually groping after the ideal and doing nothing with the positive. It was for us to carry out everything to perfection. Show me where we can make a single improvement and you shall become a prince."

"If my life depended on that, my head would be off this instant," was the quick-witted reply of the Englishman.

This so pleased the king that he laughed till he shook. "Well said," he smiled; "so you like our country?"

"Absolutely charmed; my friend (Thorndyke was determined to bring his companion into favor, if possible) and I have been in raptures ever since we rose this morning."

A flush of pleasure crossed the face of the king. "You have not seen half of our wonders yet. I confess that I am pleased with you, sir. The majority of people who are brought here are so frightened that they grow morbid and desirous to return to their own countries as soon as they learn that such a thing is out of the question."

Thorndyke's stout heart suffered a sudden pang at the words, but he did not change countenance in the slightest, for the king was closely watching the effect of his announcement.

"Of course," went on the ruler, gratified by the indifference of the Englishman, "of course, it could not be done. No one, outside of a few of the royal family and our trusted agents, has ever left us."

"I can't see how anyone could be so unappreciative as to want to go," answered Thorndyke, with a coolness that surprised even Johnston. "I have travelled in all countries under the sun--the sun I was born under--and got so bored with them that my friend and myself took to ballooning for diversion; but here, there is a delightful surprise at every turn."

"I was told you were aeronauts," returned the ruler, deigning to cast a glance at the silent Johnston, who stood with eyes downcast, "and I confess that it interested me in you."

At that juncture a most beautiful girl glided through the curtains at the back of the throne and came impulsively toward the king. Her brown hair fell in rich masses on her bare shoulders; her eyes were large, deep and brown, and her skin was exquisitely fine in texture and color; her dress was artistic and well suited to her lithe figure. She held an instrument resembling a lute in her hands, and stopped suddenly when she noticed that the king was engaged.

"It is my daughter, the Princess Bernardino," explained the king, as he heard her light step and turned toward her; "she shall sing for you, and, yes (nodding to her) you shall dance also."

As she took her position on a great rug in front of the throne, she kept her eyes on the handsome Englishman as if fascinated by his appearance. Thorndyke's heart beat quickly; the blood mantled his face and he stood entranced as she touched the resonant strings with her white fingers and began to play and sing. An innocent, artless smile parted her lips from her matchless teeth, and her face glowed with inspiration. Far above in the nooks and crannies of the vast dome, with its divergent corridors and arcades, the faint echoes of her voice seemed to reply to her during the pauses in her song. Then she ceased singing and to the far-away and yet distinct accompaniment of some stringed instrument in the orchestra, she began to dance. Holding her instrument in a graceful fashion against her shoulder as one holds a violin, and with her flowing white gown caught in the other hand, she bowed and smiled and instantly seemed transformed. From the statuesque and dreamy singer she became a marvel of graceful motion. To and fro she swept from end to end of the great rug, her tiny feet and slim ankles tripping so lightly that she seemed to move without support through the air.

Thorndyke stood as if spell-bound, for, at every turn, as if seeking his approval, she glanced at him inquiringly. When she finished she stood for a moment in the center of the rug panting, her beautiful bosom, beneath its filmy covering of lace, gently rising and falling. Then, asking her father's consent with a mute glance, she ran forward impulsively, and, kneeling at Thorndyke's feet, she took his hand and pressed it to her lips. And rising, suffused with blushes, she tripped from the dais and disappeared behind the curtain.

The king frowned as he looked after her. "It is a mark of preference," he said coldly. "It is one of our customs for a dancer or singer to favor some one of her spectators in that way. My daughter evidently mistook you for an ambassador from one of my provinces, but it does not matter."

"She is wonderfully beautiful," replied the tactful Englishman, pretending not to be flattered by the notice of the princess.

"Do you think our people fine looking as a rule?" asked the king, to change the subject.

"Decidedly; I never imagined such a race existed."

Again the king was pleased. "That is one of the objects of our system. Generation after generation we improve mentally and physically. We are the only people who have ever attempted to thoroughly study the science of living. Your medical men may be numbered by the million; your remedies for your ills change daily; what you say is good for the health today is tomorrow believed to be poison; to-day you try to make blood to give strength, and half a century ago you believed in taking it from the weakest of your patients. With all this fuss over health, you will think nothing of allowing the son of a man who died with a loathsome hereditary disease to marry a woman whose family has never had a taint of blood. Here no such thing is thought of. To begin with, no person who is not thoroughly sound can remain with us. Every heart-beat is heard by our medical men and every vein is transparent. You see evidences of the benefit of our system in the men and women around you. All our conveniences, the excellence of our products, our great inventions are the result."

"I have been wondering about the size of your country," ventured Thorndyke cautiously.

The king smiled. "That will be one of the things for you to discover later," he returned. "But this, the City of Moron, is the capital; our provinces, farming lands, smaller cities, towns and hamlets lie around us. Come with me and I will show you something."

He waved his hand and dismissed a number of courtiers who were waiting to be called, and rose from the throne and led the two captives into a large apartment adjoining the throne-room. Here they found six men in blue uniforms looking into a large circular mirror on a table. They all bowed and moved aside as the king approached.

"These men are the municipal police," explained the king, resting his hand on the gold frame of the glass; "they are watching the city." And when the strangers drew nearer they were surprised to see reflected, in the deeply concave glass, the entire city in miniature; its streets, parks, public buildings, and moving populace. And what seemed to be the most remarkable feature of the invention was, that the instant the eye rested on any particular portion of the whole that part was at once magnified so that every detail of it was clearly observable.

"This is an improvement on your police system," continued the king. "No sooner does anything go wrong than a red signal is given on the spot of the trouble and the attention of these officers is immediately called to it. A flying machine is sent out and the offender is brought to the police station; but trouble of any nature rarely occurs, and the duties of our police are merely nominal; my people live in thorough harmony. Now, come with me and I will give you an idea of the surrounding country."

As the king spoke he led them into a circular room, the roof of which was of white glass, and the walls were lined with large mirrors.

"This is our general observatory from which every part of Alpha can be seen," said the king with a touch of pride in his tone. "Look at the mirror in front of you."

They did as he requested, and at first saw nothing; but, as he went to a stone table in the center of the room and touched an electric button, a grand view of green fields, forests, streams, lakes and farm-houses flashed upon the mirror. The king laughed at their surprise and touched another button. As he did so the scene shifted gradually; the landscapes ran by like a panorama. A pretty village came into sight, and passed; then a larger town and still a larger; then fields, hills and valleys and forests of giant trees.

"It is that way all over my kingdom," said the king; "in an hour I can inspect it all."

"But how is it done?" asked Thorndyke, forgetting himself in wonder.

"Through a telescopic invention, aided by electricity and the clearness of our atmosphere," replied the king. "It would take too long to go into the details. The views, however, are reflected to this point from various observatories throughout the land. Such a system would be impossible in any other country on account of the clouds and atmospheric changes; but here we control everything."

"I noticed," returned the Englishman, "that green fields lie beside ripening ones and those in which the grain is being harvested."

"We have no change of seasons," answered the king. "Change of seasons may be according to nature, but it is in the province of man's intellect to improve on nature. But I must leave you now; I shall summon you again when I have the leisure to continue our conversation."

"Well, what do you think of it?" asked Johnston, as the king disappeared behind a curtain in the direction of the audience chamber.

"I give it up; I only know that the old fellow's daughter, the Princess Bernardino is the most beautiful, the most bewitching creature that ever breathed. Did you notice her eyes and form? Great heavens! Was there ever such a vision of human loveliness? Her grace, her voice, her glances drove me wild with delight."

"You are dead gone," grumbled the American despondently; "we'll never get away from here in the world. I can see that."

"I gave up all hope in that direction some time ago," said Thorndyke; "and why should we care? We were awfully bored with life before we came; for my part I'd as soon end mine up here as anywhere else. Besides, didn't his majesty say that they live longer under his system than we do?"

"I don't take stock in all he says," growled the American; "he talks like a Chicago real estate agent who wants to sell a lot. Why doesn't he chop off our heads and be done with it?"

Thorndyke burst into a jovial laugh. "You are coming round all right; that is the first joke you have got off since we came here; his royal Nibs may need a court-jester and give you a job."

"There goes that blamed sunlight again," exclaimed Johnston, grasping his companion's arm, "don't you see it changing?"

"Yes, and this time it is white, like old Sol's natural smile; but isn't it clear? It seems to me that I could see to the end of the earth in that light. I want to know how he does it."

"How who does it?"

"Why, the king, of course, it is his work--some sort of invention; but we must keep civil tongues in our heads when we are dealing with a man who can color the very light of the sun."

They were walking back toward the great rotunda, and, as they entered the conservatory, the crowds of men and women stared at them curiously. They had paused to inspect the statue of a massive stone dragon when a young officer in glittering uniform approached and addressed Johnston.

"Follow me," he said simply; "it is the king's command."

The American started and looked at Thorndyke apprehensively.

"Go," said the latter; "don't hesitate an instant."

Poor Johnston had turned white. He held out his hand to Thorndyke, "Shake," he said in a whisper, not intended for the ears of the officer, "I don't believe that we shall meet again. I felt that we were to be parted ever since that medical examination."

Thorndyke's face had altered; an angry flush came in his face and his eyes flashed, but with an effort he controlled himself.

"Tut, tut, don't be silly. I shall wait for you round here; if there is any foul play I shall make someone suffer for it. You can depend on me to the end; we are hand in hand in this adventure, old man."

Chapter VII

Johnston followed his guide to a flying machine outside. He hesitated an instant, as the officer was holding the door open, and looked back toward the conservatory; but he could not see Thorndyke.

"Where are you taking me?" he asked desperately. But the officer did not seem to hear the question. He was motioning to a tall man of athletic build who wore a dark blue uniform and who came hastily forward and pushed the American into the machine. Through the open door Johnston saw Thorndyke's anxious face as the Englishman emerged from the conservatory and strode toward them. The two officers entered and closed the glass door.

Then the machine rose and Johnston's spirits sank as they shot upward and floated easily over the humming crowd into the free white light above the smokeless city. The poor captive leaned on the window-sill and looked out. There was no breeze, and no current of air except that caused by their rapid passage through the atmosphere.

Up, up, they went, till the city seemed a blur of mingled white and gray, and then the color below changed to a vague blue as they flew over the fields of the open country.

The first officer took a glass and a decanter from a receptacle under a seat, and, pouring a little red fluid into the glass, offered it to the American.

"Drink it," he said, "it will put you to sleep for a time."

"I don't want to be drugged."

"The journey will try your nerves. It is harmless."

"I don't want it; if I take it, you will have to pour it down my throat."

The officer smiled as he put the glass and decanter away. Faster and faster flew the machine. They had to put the window down, for the current of air had become too strong and cool to be pleasant. The color of the sunlight changed to green, and then at noon, from the zenith, a glorious red light shimmered down and veiled the earth with such a beautiful translucent haze that the poor American for a moment almost forgot his trouble.

The afternoon came on. The sunlight became successively green, white, blue, lavender, rose and gray. The sun was no longer in sight and the gray in the west was darkening into purple, the last hour of the day. Night was at hand. Johnston's limbs were growing stiff from inaction, and he had a strong desire to speak or to hear one of the officers say something, but they were dozing in their respective corners. The moon had risen and hung far out in space overhead, but they seemed to be leaving it behind. Later he felt sure of this, for its light gradually became dimmer and dimmer till at last they were in total darkness--darkness pierced only by the powerful search-light which threw its dazzling, trumpet-shaped rays far ahead. But, search as he would in the direction they were going, the unfortunate American could see nothing but the ever-receding wall of blackness.

Suddenly they began to descend. The officers awoke and stretched themselves and yawned. One of them opened the window and Johnston heard a far-off, roaring sound like that of a multitude of skaters on a vast sheet of ice.

Down, down, they dropped. Johnston's heart was in his mouth.

The machine suddenly slackened in its speed and then hung poised in mid-air. The rays of the search-light were directed downward and slowly shifted from point to point. Looking down, the American caught glimpses of rugged rocks, sharp cliffs and yawning chasms.

"How is it?" asked the first officer, through a speaking-tube, of the driver.

"A good landing!" was the reply.

"Well, go down." And a moment later the machine settled on the uneven ground.

The same officer opened the door, and gently pushed Johnston out. Johnston expected them to follow him, but the door of the machine closed behind him.

"Stand out of the way," cried out the officer through the window; "you may get struck as we rise."

Involuntarily Johnston obeyed. There was a sound of escaping air from beneath the machine, a fierce commotion in the atmosphere which sucked him toward the machine, and then the dazzling search-light blinded him, as the air-ship bounded upward and sailed back over the course it had come.

Johnston stood paralyzed with fear. "My God, this is awful!" he exclaimed in terror, and his knees gave way beneath him and he sank to the rock. "They have left me here to starve in this hellish darkness!" He remained there for a moment, his face covered with his hands, then he sprang up desperately, and started to grope through the darkness, he knew not whither. He stumbled at almost every step, and ran against boulders which bruised his hands and face, and went on till his strength was gone. Then he paused and looked back toward the direction from which he had come. It seemed to him that he could see the straight line of mighty black wall above which there was a faint appearance of light. A lump rose in the throat of the poor fellow, and tears sprang into his eyes.

But what was that? Surely it was a sound. It could not have been the wind, for the air was perfectly still. The sound was repeated. It was like the moaning of a human voice far away in the dark. Could it be someone in distress, some poor unfortunate, banished being, like himself? Again he heard the sound, and this time, it was like the voice of someone talking.

"Hello!" shouted the American, and a cold shudder went over him at the sound of his own husky voice. There was a dead silence, then, like an echo of his own cry, faintly came the word, "Hello!"

Filled with superstitious fear, the American cautiously groped toward the sound. "Hello, there, who are you?"

"Help, help!" said the voice, and it was now much nearer.

Johnston plunged forward precipitately. "Where are you?"

"Here," and a human form loomed up before him.

For a moment neither spoke, then the strange figure said: "I thought at first that you were some one sent to rescue me, but I see you are alone--damned like myself."

"It looks that way," replied Johnston.

"When did they bring you?"

"Only a moment ago."

"My God, it is awful! A week ago I did not dream of such a fate as this. I had enemies. The medical men were bribed to vote against me. Am I not strong? Am I not muscular? Feel my arms and thighs."

He held out an arm and Johnston felt of it. The muscles were like stone.

"You are a giant."

"Ah! You are right; but they reported that there was a taint in my blood. I was to marry Lallio, the most beautiful creature in our village--Madryl, you know, the nearest hamlet to the home of the Sun. I was rich, and the best farmer there. But Lyngale wanted her. She hated him and spat at him when he spoke against me. He proved by others that my lungs were weak, and showed them the blood of a slain dog in my fields that they said had come from my lungs. Ah, they were curs! My lungs weak! Strike my chest with all your might. Does it not sound like the king's thunder? Strike, I say!" and as the enfeebled American struck his bare breast he cried:--"Harder, harder! Pooh, you are a child, see this, and this," and he emphasized his words with thunderous blows on his resounding chest.

"But it has been so for a century," he panted; "hundreds have been unjustly buried alive here. The king thinks it is not murder because they die of starvation. I have stumbled over the bones of giants here in the dark lands, and have met dying men that are stronger than the king's athletes."

"What, are there others here?" gasped the American.

The Alphian was silent in astonishment.

"Why, where did you come from?" he asked, after a pause.

"From New York City."

"I don't know of it, and yet I thought I knew of all the places inside the great endless wall."

Johnston was mystified in his turn. "It is not in your country—your world, or whatever you call it. It is far away."

"Ah, under the white sun! In the 'Ocean Country,' and the world of fierce winds and disease. And you are from there. I had heard of it before they banished me; but two days since I came across a dying man, away over there. He was huddled against the wall, and had fallen and killed himself in his efforts to climb back to food and light.

"I saw him die. He told me that he had come from your land when he was a child. His trouble was the lungs and he had fallen off to a skeleton. He talked to me of your wide ocean land. Is it, indeed so great? And has it no walls about it?"

"No, it is surrounded by water."

"I cannot understand," and, after a pause, in which Johnston could hear the great fellow's heart beating, he continued; "That must be the Heaven the man spoke about. And beyond the water is it always dark like this, and do they banish people there as the king has us?"

"No; beyond are other countries. But is there no chance for us to escape from here?"

The Alphian laughed bitterly. "None. What were you banished for?"

"I hardly know."

"Hold out your arm. There," as he grasped Johnston's arm in a clasp of iron, "I see; you are undeveloped, unfit--none but the healthy and strong are allowed to live in Alpha. It is right, of course; but it is hard to bear. But I must lie down. I am wearied with constant rambling. I am nervous too. I fell asleep a while ago and dreamt I heard all my friends in a great clamoring body calling my name, 'Branasko!' and then I awoke and cried for help."

As he spoke he sank with a sigh to the ground and rested his head on his elbows and knees and seemed asleep. The American sat down beside him, and, for a long time, neither spoke. Branasko broke the silence; he awoke with a start and eyed his companion in sleepy wonder.

"Ugh, I dreamt again," he grunted, "Are you asleep?"

"No," was Johnston's reply. "I am hungry and thirsty and cannot sleep."

"So am I, but we must wait till it is lighter, then we can go in search of food. When I was a boy I learned to catch fish in pools with my hands and it has prolonged my life here. When the light comes again, I shall show you how I do it."

"Then the day does break? I thought it was eternally dark here."

"It does not get very light, because we are behind the sun; but it is lighter than now, for we get the sun's reflection, enough at least to keep us from falling into the chasms."

Branasko lowered his head to his knees and slept again, but the American, though wearied, was wakeful. Several hours passed. The Alphian was sleeping soundly, his breathing was very heavy and he had rolled down on his side.

Far away in the east the darkness gradually faded into purple, and then into gray, and slowly hints of pink appeared in the skies. It was dawn. Johnston touched his companion. The man awoke and looked at him from his great swollen eyes.

"It is day," he yawned, rising and stretching himself.

"But the sun is not in sight."

"No; it shows itself only in the middle of the day, and then but for a few minutes. We must go now and search for food. I will show you how to catch the eyeless fish in the black caverns over there." And he led the American into the blackness behind them. Every now and then, as they stumbled along, Johnston would look longingly back toward the faint pink light that shone above the high black wall. But Branasko hastened on.

Presently they came to the edge of a black chasm and the American was filled with awe, for, from the seemingly fathomless depths, came a great roaring sound like that of a mighty wind and the air that came from it was hot, though pure and free from the odor of gas.

"What is this?" he asked.

"They are everywhere," answered Branasko, "if it were not for their hot breathing the Land of the Changing Sun would be cold and damp."

"Then the sun does not give out heat?"

"No."

"It is cold?"

"I believe so, I have never thought much about it."

The American was mystified, but he did not question farther, for Branasko was carefully lowering himself into the hot gulf.

"Follow me," he said; "we must cross it to reach the caves. I will guide you. I have been over this way before."

"But can we stand the heat?"

"Oh, yes; when we get used to it, it is invigorating. I perspire in streams, but I feel better afterward. Come on."

Branasko's head only was above the ground. "I am standing on a ledge," he said. "Get down beside me. Fear nothing. It is solid; besides, what does it matter? You can die but once, and it would really be better to fall down there into the internal fires than to starve slowly."

Johnston shuddered convulsively as he let himself down beside Branasko. His foot dislodged a stone. With a crash it fell upon a lower ledge and bounded off and went whizzing down into the depths. Both men listened. They heard the stone bounding from ledge to ledge till the sound was lost in the internal roaring.

"It is mighty deep," said Johnston.

"Yes, but follow me; we cannot stop here; we must go along this ledge till we get to the point where the chasm is narrow enough to jump across. I have done it."

"The American held to his companion with one hand and the rock with the other, and they slowly made their way along the narrow ledge, pausing every now and then to rest. At every step the path grew more perilous and narrower, and the cliff on their left rose higher and higher, till the reflected light of the sun had entirely disappeared. At certain points the hot wind dashed upon them as furiously as the whirling mist in 'The Cave of Winds' at Niagara Falls. Once Johnston's foot slipped and he fell, but was drawn back to safety by the strong arm of the Alphian.

"Be careful; hold to the cliff's face," warned Branasko indifferently, and he moved onward as if nothing unusual had occurred. Presently they reached a point where a narrow boulder jutted out over the chasm toward the opposite side, and Branasko cautiously crawled out upon it. When he had got to its end, Johnston could not see him in the gloom, but his voice came to him out of the roaring of the chasm.

"I can see the other side, and am going to jump." An instant later, the American heard the clatter of the Alphian's shoes on the rock, and his grunt of satisfaction. Then Branasko called out: "Come on; crawl out till you feel the end of the rock, and then you can see me."

In great trepidation the American slowly crawled out on the narrow rock. Below him yawned the hot darkness, above hung that black ominous canopy of nothingness. Slowly he advanced on hands and knees, every moment feeling the sharp rock growing narrower, till finally he reached the end. He looked ahead. He could but faintly see the ledge and Branasko's tall form silhouetted upon it.

"See, this is where you have to alight," cried the Alphian. "Jump, I will catch you!"

"I am afraid I shall topple over when I stand up," replied the American.
"The rock is narrow and my head is already swimming. I fear I cannot reach you. It is no use."

"Tut, tut!" exclaimed Branasko. "Stand up quickly, and jump at once. Don't stop to think about it."

Johnston obeyed. He felt his feet firmly braced on the rock and he sprang toward the opposite ledge with all his might. Branasko caught him.

"Good," he grunted. "There is another place, we must jump again. It is further on." Along this ledge they went for some distance, Branasko leading the way and holding the arm of the American.

"Now here we are, the chasm is a little wider, but the ledge on the other side is broader." As he spoke he released Johnston's arm and prepared to jump. He filled his lungs two or three times. But he seemed to hesitate. "Pshaw, watching you back there has made me nervous. I never cared before. If I should happen to fall, go back to where we met, it is safer there without a guide than here."

Without another word Branasko hurled himself forward. Johnston held his breath in horror, for Branasko's foot had slipped as he jumped. The Alphian had struck the opposite ledge, but not with his feet, as he intended. He clutched it with his hands and hung there for a moment, struggling to get a foothold in the emptiness beneath him.

"It's no use, I am falling; I can hold no longer!" And Johnston,--too terrified to reply,--heard the poor fellow's hands slipping from the rock, causing a quantity of loose stones to go rattling down below. With a low cry Branasko fell. An instant later Johnston heard him strike the ledge beneath, and heard him cry out in pain. Then all was still except the echoes of Branasko's cry, which bounded and rebounded from side to side of the chasm, and grew fainter and fainter, till it was submerged in the roaring below. Then there was a rattle of stones, and Branasko's voice sounded: "A narrow escape!" he said faintly. "I am on another ledge"--then after a slight pause, "it is much wider, I don't know how wide. Are you listening?"

"Yes, but are you hurt?"

"Not at all. Simply knocked the breath out of me for a moment. There is a cave behind me, and (for a moment there was silence) I can see a light ahead in the cave. I think it must be the reflection of the internal fire. Come down to me and we will explore the cavern, and see where the light comes from."

"I can't get down there!" shouted Johnston, to make himself heard above a sudden increase in the roaring in the chasm, "there is no way."

"Wait a moment!" came from the Alphian. "This ledge seems to incline upward."

Johnston stood perfectly motionless, afraid to move from the ledge either to right or to left, and heard Branasko's footsteps along the rock beneath. "All right so far," he called up, and his voice showed that he had gone to a considerable distance to the left, "the ledge seems to be still leading gradually upward. I think I can reach you."

Fifteen minutes passed. The lone American could no longer hear Branasko's footsteps. Johnston was becoming uneasy and the hot air was causing his head to swim. He was thinking of trying to retrace his footsteps to a place of more security when he heard footsteps, and then the cheery voice of Branasko nearly opposite him across the chasm:

"Are you there?"

"Yes."

"It is well; I have discovered a good pathway down to the cave, and a pool of fish besides. I have saved some for you. I was so hungry I had to eat. Now, you must jump over to me."

"I cannot," declared the American. "I cannot jump so far; besides, you failed."

Branasko laughed. "I did not leap in the right direction. It is this point on which I am now standing that I should have tried to reach. Come, I will catch you."

Johnston could not bear to be considered cowardly, so he stepped to the verge of the chasm and prepared to jump. His head felt more dizzy as he thought of the fathomless depths beneath, and the rush of hot air up the side of the cliff took his breath away, but he braced himself and said calmly: "All right, I am coming." The next instant he sprang forward. Branasko caught him into his arms and they both rolled back on the level stone.

"Good," cried the Alphian, trying to catch his breath, which Johnston had knocked out of him by the fall. "You did better than I; you are lighter."

"Where shall we go now?" asked Johnston, regaining his feet and feeling of his legs and arms to see if he had broken any bones.

"Down this winding path to the place where I saw that light. I want to understand it. But you must first eat this fish. It is delicious. They are swarming in the pools below."

"And water?" said Johnston.

"An abundance of it, and as cold as ice."

As Branasko preceded him down the tortuous path, Johnston ate the raw fish eagerly. Presently they came to a deep pool of water, and both men threw themselves down on their stomachs and drank freely. After this they proceeded slowly for several hundred yards, and finally reached the entrance to the cave in which Branasko had seen the light. At that distance it looked like the light of some great conflagration reflected from the face of a cliff.

They entered the cave and made good progress toward the light, for it showed them the dangerous fissures, sharp boulders and stalactites. They had walked along in silence for several minutes when the Alphian stopped abruptly and turned to his companion. "What is the matter?" asked Johnston.

"It cannot come from the internal fires," replied Branasko, "for the atmosphere grows cooler as we get nearer the light and away from the chasm."

Johnston was too much puzzled to formulate a reply, and he simply waited for the Alphian to continue.

"Let's go on," said Branasko; and in his tone and hesitating manner Johnston detected the first appearance of superstitious fear that he had seen in the brawny Alphian.

Chapter VIII

As Thorndyke watched the flying machine that was bearing his friend away a genuine feeling of pity went over him. Poor Johnston! He had been haunted all day with the belief that he was to meet with some misfortune from which Thorndyke was to be spared, and Thorndyke had ridiculed his fears. When the airship had become a mere speck in the sky, the Englishman turned back into the palace and strolled about in the vast crowd.

A handsome young man in uniform approached and touched his hat:

"Are you the comrade of the fellow they are just sending away?" he asked.

"Yes. Where are they taking him?"

"To the 'Barrens,' of course; where do you suppose they would take such a man? He couldn't pass his examination. You are not a great physical success yourself, but they say you pleased the king with your tongue."

"To the Barrens," repeated Thorndyke, too much concerned over the fate of his comrade to notice the speaker's tone of contempt; "what are they, where are they?"

The Alphian officer changed countenance, as he looked him over with widening eyes.

"Your accent is strange; are you from the other world?"

"I suppose so,--this is a new one to me at any rate."

"The world of endless oceans?"

"Yes."

"And the unchanging sun--forever white and----?"

"Yes; but where the devil is the Barrens?"

"Behind the sun, beyond the great endless wall."

"Do they intend to put him to death?"

"No, that would be--what do you call it? Murder; they will simply leave him there to die of his own accord. And the king is right. I never saw such a weakling. He would taint our whole race with his presence."

Without a word Thorndyke abruptly turned from the officer and hastened toward the apartment of the king. He would demand the return of poor Johnston or kill the king if his demand was not granted. In his haste and perturbation, however, he lost his way and wandered into a part of the palace he had not seen. At every step he was more and more impressed with the magnificent proportions of the structure and the grandeur of everything about it.

Passing hurriedly through a large hall he saw an assemblage of beautiful women and handsome men dancing to the music of a great orchestra. Further on--in a great court--a regiment of soldiers were drilling, their rapid evolutions making no more sound than if they were moving in mid-air. In another room he saw a great body of men, women and children in vari-colored suits bathing in a pool of rose-colored, perfumed water.

He was passing on when a woman, closely veiled and simply dressed, touched his arm.

"Be watchful and follow me," she said, in a low, guarded tone.

The heart of the Englishman bounded and his blood rushed to his face, for the speaker was the Princess Bernardino. She did not pause, but glided on into the shade of a great palm tree, and, behind a row of thick-growing ferns of great height and thickness, she waited for him.

She lowered her veil as he approached and looked at him from her deep brown eyes in great concern. He stood spell-bound under the witchery of her beauty.

"I came to warn you, Prince," she said, and her soft musical voice set every nerve in Thorndyke's body to tingling with delight. "My father has banished the faithful slave that you love, but you must not show the anger that you feel, else he will kill you. You must be exceedingly cautious if you would save him. My father would punish me severely if he knew that I had sought you in this way. I was obliged to come in disguise; this dress belongs to my most trusted maid."

"And you came for my sake?" blurted out the Englishman, much embarrassed; "I am not worthy of such a high honor."

She smiled and tears rose in her eyes.

"Oh, Prince, don't speak to me so! You are far above me. I am weak. I know nothing. I never cared for other men than the king and my brothers till I saw you today, but now I would willingly be your slave."

"I am yours forever, and a humble one," bowed the courteous Englishman. "The moment I saw you at the throne of your father my heart went out to you. You wound it up in your music and trampled it under your dancing feet. I have been over the whole world, and you are the loveliest creature in it. It is because I saw you, because you are here, that I do not want to leave your country. They may do as they will with me if they only will let me see you now and then."

The princess was deeply moved. The blood rushed to her face and beautified it. Her eyes fell beneath his admiring glance. Thorndyke could not restrain himself. He caught her slender hand and pressed it passionately to his lips, and she made only a slight effort to prevent it.

"I am your obedient slave; what shall I do?" he asked.

"Do not try to rescue him now," she said softly. "I shall come to you again when we are not watched--you can know me by this dress. There is no need for great haste, he could live in the Barrens several days; I shall try to think of some way to save him, though such a thing has never been done--never."

Footsteps were heard on the other side of the row of ferns. A man was passing and others soon followed him. The bathers were leaving the great pool.

"I must leave you now," she whispered. "If the king honors you again by talking of his kingdom, continue to act as you did; your fearlessness and good humor have pleased him greatly."

"Could I not persuade him to bring Johnston back?"

"No; that would be impossible; those who are pronounced physically unfit are obliged to die. It has been a law for a long time; you must not count on that. I have, however, another plan, but I cannot tell you of it now, for they may miss me and wonder where I am, and then, too, my father may be looking for you. He will naturally desire to see you soon again."

Bowing, she turned away and passed on toward the apartments of the king, which the Englishman now recognized in the distance. Thorndyke went into the bathing-room to watch those remaining in the great pool of rose-colored water. The sight was beautiful. The waves which lapped against the shelving shores of white marble were pink and white, and the deeper water was as red as coral.

The Englishman was at once troubled over the fate of Johnston and elated over having won Bernardino's regard. Thoughtfully he strolled away from the bathers into a great picture-gallery. Here hung on the walls and stood on pedestals some of the rarest works of art he had ever seen. He passed through this room and was entering a shady retreat where plants, flowers and umbrageous trees grew thickly, when he heard a step behind him and the rustling of a silken skirt against the plants.

It was Bernardino.

"We can be unobserved here," she said, taking off her thick veil and arranging her luxuriant hair. "I hasten back. The king thinks, so my maid tells me, that I am asleep in my chamber. He is busy with an audience of police from a neighboring town and will not think of us."

She sat down on a sofa upholstered in leather, and he took a seat beside her. "I am glad that we can talk alone," he said, "for I have much to ask you. First, tell me where we are,--where this strange country is on the map of the world."

"It is a long story," she replied, "and it would greatly incense the king if he should find out that I had told you, for one of his chief pleasures is to note the surprise and admiration of newcomers over what they see here.

But if you will promise to gratify his vanity in this particular I will try to explain it all."

"I promise, and you can depend on my not getting you into trouble," replied Thorndyke. "I never was so puzzled in my life, with that sullen sky overhead, the wonderful changing sunlight, and the remarkable atmosphere. I am both bewildered and entranced. Every moment I see something new and startling. Where are we?"

"Far beneath the ocean and the surface of the earth. I only know what the king has let fall in my hearing in his conferences with his men of science and inventors; but I shall try to make you understand how it all came about."

"It was a long time ago, two hundred years back, I suppose, that one of my ancestors discovered a little isolated island in the Atlantic Ocean. He was forced in a storm to land there with his ship and crew to make some repairs in his vessel. In wandering about over the island he discovered a narrow entrance to a cave, and, with two or three of his men, he began to explore it. When they had gone for a mile or two down into the interior of the cavern, which seemed to lead straight down toward the center of the earth, they began to find small pieces of gold. The further they went the more they found, till at last the very cavern walls seemed lined with it.

"They were at first wildly excited over their sudden good fortune and were about to load their ship with it and return to Europe at once, but the better judgment of my ancestor prevailed. He explained that, if the world were informed of the discovery of such an inexhaustible mine of gold, that the value of the precious metal would decline till it would be worth little more than some grosser metal, and that if they would only keep their secret to themselves they could in time control the finances of the world. So, acting on this suggestion, they only dug out a few thousand pounds and took part of it to Europe and part of it to America and turned it into money.

"Then, to curtail my story, they elected my ancestor as ruler, and, with ships loaded with every available convenience that inexhaustible wealth could procure and a colony of carefully chosen men, they returned to the island.

"After the men and their families had settled in the great roomy mouth of the cavern my ancestor supplied himself with several strong men and food and lights, and sought to explore the entire cavern.

"To their astonishment they found that it was practically endless. When they had gone down about sixty or seventy miles below the sea level they found themselves on a vast, undulating plain, the soil of which was dark and rich, with the black roof of the cavern arching overhead like the bottom of a great inverted bowl. And when they had travelled about ten days and reached the other side my ancestor calculated that the cave must be over one hundred miles in diameter and almost circular in shape. But what elated and surprised them most was the remarkable salubrity of the atmosphere. In all parts of the cave it was exactly the same temperature, and they found that they scarcely felt any fatigue from their journey, and that they had little desire to eat the provisions with which they were supplied. Indeed, the very air seemed permeated with a subtle quality that gave them strength and energy of mind and body.

"Finally, when, after a month had passed, and they returned to their anxious friends, these people overwhelmed them with exclamations of surprise over their appearance. And in the light of day the explorers looked at one another in astonishment, for, in the dim light of the lanterns they had carried, they had not noticed the great change that had come over them. They had all become the finest specimens of physical health that could be imagined. Their bodies had filled out; they were remarkably strong; their skins shone with healthful color and their eyes sparkled with intellectual energy, and their minds, even to the humblest burden-carrier, were astonishingly acute and active.

"My ancestor was a remarkable man, and he had hitherto shown much inventive ability; but in that month in the cave he had developed into an intellectual giant. After mature deliberation, he proposed a prodigious scheme to his followers. He explained that, while they might, by using the utmost discretion, hold the financial world in their power by means of their inexhaustible wealth, that the laws and restrictions of different countries prevented men of vast wealth from really enjoying more privileges than men of moderate means. He grew eloquent in speaking of the underground atmosphere, and proposed that they light the great cavern from end to end and make it an ideal place where they could live as it suited them.

"I see that you guess the end. My ancestor was a great student of the sciences and had already thought of putting electricity to practical use. You are surprised? Yes, it has been applied to our purposes for two hundred years, while your people have understood its use such a short time."

"Great heavens!" exclaimed the Englishman. "I see it all; the sun is an electric one!"

"Yes."

"And it runs mechanically over its great course as regularly as clock-work."

"More accurately, I assure you, but there probably never was a greater mathematical problem than they solved in deciding on the size the sun should be and amount of light necessary to fill up all the recesses of the great vacancy. It was all very crude at the start; for years a great electric light was simply suspended in the center of the cavern's roof and the light did not vary in color. A son of the first king suggested the plan of giving the sun diurnal movement and the changing light. The moon and stars were a later development. They found, too, that the light could not be made to reach certain recesses in the cavern where the roof approached the earth, so they finally built a great wall to keep the inhabitants within proscribed boundaries, and to prevent them from understanding the machinery of the heavens."

"Wonderful!" exclaimed Thorndyke. "But the temperature of the atmosphere, how does that happen to be so delightful and beneficial?"

"I believe they do not themselves thoroughly comprehend that. The heat comes from the internal fires, and the fresh air from without in some mysterious way. At first, in a few places, the heat was too severe, but the scientific men among the first settlers obviated this difficulty by closing up the hottest of the fissures and opening others in the cooler parts of the cavern."

"And the people, where did they come from?"

"From all parts of the earth. We had agents outside who selected such men and women that were willing to come, and who filled all the requirements, mentally and physically."

"But why do they desire to live here instead of out in the world, when they have all the wealth that they need to assure every advantage."

"They dread death, and it is undoubtedly true that life is prolonged here; our medical men declare that the longevity of every generation is improved."

"Is it possible? But tell me about the sun, when it sets, what becomes of it?"

"It goes back to its place of rising through a great tunnel beneath us."

Thorndyke sat in deep thought for a moment; then he looked so steadily and so admiringly into Bernardino's eyes that she grew red with confusion. "But you, yourself, are you thoroughly content here?"

"I know nothing else," she continued. "I have heard little about your world except that your people are discontented, weak and insane, and that your changeable weather and your careless laws regarding marriage and heredity produce perpetual and innumerable diseases; that your people are not well developed and beautiful; that you war with one another, and that one tears down what another builds. I have, too, always been happy, and since you came I am happier still. I don't know what it means. I have never been so much interested in any one before."

"It is love on the part of both of us," replied the Englishman impulsively, taking her hand. "I never was content before. I went roving over the earth trying to end my life at sea or in balloon voyages, but now I only want to be with you. I have never dreamed that I could be so happy or that I would meet any one so beautiful as you are."

Bernardino's delight showed itself in blushes on her face, and Thorndyke, unable to restrain himself, put his arm around her and drew her to his breast and kissed her.

She sprang up quickly and he saw that she was trembling and that all the color had fled from her face.

"What is the matter?" he asked, in alarm.

At first she did not answer, but only looked at him half-frightened, and then covered her face with her hands. He drew them from her face and compelled her to look at him.

"What is the matter?" he repeated, a strange fear at his heart.

"You have broken one of the most sacred laws of our country," she faltered, in great embarrassment; "my father would punish me very severely if he knew of it, and he would banish you; for, to treat me in that manner, as his daughter, is regarded as an insult to him."

"I beg your pardon most humbly," said the contrite Englishman. "It was all on account of my ignorance of your customs and my impulsiveness. It shall never happen again, I promise you."

Her face brightened a little and the color came back slowly. She sat down again, but not so near Thorndyke, and seemed desirous of changing the subject.

"And do you love the man my father has transported?" she questioned.

"Yes, he is a good, faithful fellow, and it is hard to die so far away from friends."

"We must try to save him, but I cannot now think of a safe plan. The police are very vigilant."

"Where was he taken?"

"Into the darkness behind the sun--beyond the wall of which I spoke."

A flush of shame came into Thorndyke's face over the remembrance that he had made no effort to aid poor Johnston, and was sitting listening with delight to the conversation of Bernardino. He rose suddenly.

"I must be doing something to aid him," he said. "I cannot sit here inactive while he is in danger."

"Be patient," she advised, looking at him admiringly; "it is near night; see, it is the gray light of dusk; the sun is out of sight. To-night, if possible, I shall come to you. Perhaps I shall approach you without disguise if you are in the throne-room and my father does not object to my entertaining you, but for the present we must separate. Adieu."

He bowed low as she turned away, and joined the throng that was passing along outside. An officer approached him. It was Captain Tradmos, who bowed and smiled pleasantly.

"I congratulate you," he said, with suave pleasantness.

"Upon what?" Thorndyke was on his guard at once.

"Upon having pleased the king so thoroughly. No stranger, in my memory, has ever been treated so courteously. Every other new-comer is put under surveillance, but you are left unwatched."

"He is easily pleased," said the Englishman, "for I have done nothing to gratify him."

"I thought he would like you; and I felt that your friend would have to suffer, but I could not help him."

"He shall not suffer if I can prevent it."

"Sh--be cautious. Those words, implying an inclination to treason, if spoken to any other officer would place you under immediate arrest. I like you; therefore I want to warn you against such folly. You are wholly in the king's power. Another thing I would specially warn you against----"

"And that is?"

"Not to allow the king to suspect your admiration for the Princess Bernardino. It would displease the king. She is much taken with you; I saw it in her eyes when she danced for your entertainment."

Thorndyke made no reply, but gazed searchingly into the eyes of the officer. Tradmos laughed.

"You are afraid of me."

"No, I am not, I trust you wholly; I know that you are honorable; I never make a mistake along that line."

Tradmos bowed, pleased by the compliment.

"I shall aid you all I can with my advice, for I know you will not betray me; but at present I am powerless to give you material aid. Every subject of this realm is bound to the autocratic will of the king. It is impossible for anyone to get from under his power."

"Why?"

"The only outlet to the upper world is carefully guarded by men who would not be bribed."

"Is there any chance for my friend?"

"None that I can see, but I must walk on; there comes one of the king's attendants."

"The king has asked to speak to you," announced the attendant to Thorndyke.

"I will go with you," was his reply, and he followed the man through the crowded corridors into the throne-room of the king. Thorndyke forced a smile as he saw the king smiling at him as he approached the throne.

"What do you think of my palace?" asked the king, after Thorndyke had knelt before him.

"It is superb," answered the Englishman, recalling the advice of Bernardino. "I am dazed by its splendor, its architecture, and its art. I have seen nothing to equal it on earth."

The king rose and stood beside him. His manner was both pleasing and sympathetic. "I am persuaded," said he, "that you will make a good subject, and have the interest of Alpha always at heart, but I have often been mistaken in the character of men and think it best to give you a timely warning. An attendant will conduct you to a chamber beneath the palace where it will be your privilege to converse with a man who once planned to get up a rebellion among my people."

There had come suddenly a stern harshness into the king's tone that roused the fears of Thorndyke. He was about to reply, but the king held up his hand. "Wait till you have visited the dungeon of Nordeskyne, then I am sure that you will be convinced that strict obedience in thought as well as deed is best for an inhabitant of Alpha." Speaking thus, he signed to an attendant who came forward and bowed.

"Conduct him to the dungeon of Nordeskyne, and return to me," ordered the king.

Thorndyke's heart was heavy, and he was filled with strange forebodings, but he simply smiled and bowed, as the attendant led him away. The attendant opened a door at the back of the throne-room and they were confronted by darkness. They went along a narrow corridor for some distance, the darkness thickening at every step. There was no sound except the sound of the guide's shoes on the smooth stone pavement. Presently the man released Thorndyke's arm, saying:

"It is narrow here, follow close behind, and do not attempt to go back."

"I shall certainly stick to you," replied the Englishman drily. They turned a sharp corner suddenly, and were going in another direction when Thorndyke felt a soft warm hand steal into his from behind, and knew intuitively that it was Bernardino. The guide was a few feet in advance of them and she drew Thorndyke's head down and whispered into his ear.

"Be brave--by all that you love--for your life, keep your presence of mind, and----"

"What was that?" asked the guide, turning suddenly and catching the Englishman's arm, "I thought I heard whispering."

"I was saying my prayers, that is all," and the Englishman pressed the hand of the princess, who, pressed close against the wall, was gliding cautiously away.

"Prayers, humph--you'll need them later, come on!" and he caught the Englishman's arm and hastily drew him onward. Thorndyke's spirits sank lower. The air of the narrow under-ground corridor was cold and damp, and he quivered from head to foot.

Chapter IX

Branasko paused again in his walk towards the mysterious light.

"It cannot be from the internal fires," said he, "for this light is white, and the glow of the fires is red."

"Let's turn back," suggested Johnston, "it can do us no good to go down there; it is only taking us further from the wall."

"I should like to understand it," returned the Alphian thoughtfully; "and, besides, there can be no more danger there than back among the hot crevices. We have got to perish anyway, and we might as well spice the remainder of our lives with whatever adventure we can. Who knows what we may not discover? There are many things about the land of Alpha that the inhabitants do not understand."

"I'll follow you anywhere," acquiesced Johnston; "you are right."

They stumbled on over the rocky surface in silence. At times, the roof of the cavern sank so low that they had to stoop to pass under it, and again it rose sharply like the roof of a cathedral, and the rays of the far-away, but ever-increasing light, shone upon glistening stalactites that hung from the darkness above them like daggers of diamonds set in ebony.

"It is not so near as I supposed," said the Alphian wearily. "And the light seemed to me to be shining on a cliff over which water is pouring in places. Yes, you can see that it is water by the ripples in the light."

"Yes, but where can the light itself be?"

"I cannot yet tell; wait till we get nearer."

In about an hour they came to a wide chasm on the other side of which towered a vast cliff of white crystal. It was on this that the trembling light was playing.

"Not a waterfall after all," said Branasko; "See, there is the source of the reflection," and he pointed to the left through a series of dark chambers of the cavern to a dazzling light. "Come, let's go nearer it." He moved a few steps forward and then happening to look over his shoulder he stopped abruptly, and uttered an exclamation of surprise.

"What is it?" And Johnston followed the eyes of the Alphian.

"Our shadows on the crystal cliff," said Branasko in an awed tone; "only the light from the changing sun could make them so."

Johnston shuddered superstitiously at the tone of Branasko's quivering voice, and their giant shadows which stood out on the smooth crystal like silhouettes. So clear-cut were they, that, in his own shadow, the

American could see his breast heaving and in Branasko's the quivering of the Alphian's huge body and limbs.

"If we have happened upon the home of the sun, only the spirit of the dead kings could tell what will become of us," said Branasko.

"Puh! You are blindly superstitious," said Johnston; "what if we do come upon the sun? Let's go down there and look into the mystery."

Branasko fell into the rear and the American stoutly pushed ahead toward the light which was every moment increasing. As they advanced the cave got larger until it opened out into a larger plain over which hung fathomless darkness, and out of the plain a great dazzling globe of light was slowly rising.

"It is the sun itself," exclaimed Branasko, and he sank to the earth and covered his face with his hands. "I have not thought ever to see it out of the sky."

The American was deeply thrilled by the grand sight. He sat down by Branasko and together they watched the vast ball of light emerge from the black earth and gradually disappear in a great hole in the roof of the cavern. It left a broad stream of light behind it, and, now that the sun itself was out of view, the silent spectators could see the great square hole from which it had risen.

As if by mutual consent, they rose and made their way over the rocks to the verge of the hole, which seemed several thousand feet square. At first, owing to the brightness of the sun overhead, they could see nothing; but, as the great orb gradually disappeared, they began to see lights and the figures of men moving about below. Later they observed the polished parts of stupendous machinery--machinery that moved almost noiselessly.

Johnston caught sight of a great net-work of moving cables reaching from the machinery up through the hole above and exclaimed enthusiastically:--"A mechanical sun! Electric daylight! What genius! A world in a great cave! Hundreds of square miles and thousands of well-organized people living under the light of an artificial sun!"

The Alphian looked at him astonished. "Is it not so in your country?" he asked.

Johnston smiled. "The great sun that lights the outer world is as much greater than that ball of light as Alpha is greater than a grain of sand. But this surely is the greatest achievement of man. But while I now understand how your sun goes over the whole of Alpha, I cannot see how it returns."

"Then you have not heard of the great tunnel of the Sun," replied the Alphian.

"No, what is it?"

"It runs beneath Alpha and connects the rising and setting points of the sun. There is a point beneath the king's palace where, by a staircase, the king and his officers may go down and inspect the sun as it is on its way back to the east during the day."

"Wonderful!"

"And once a year a royal party goes in the sun over its entire course. It is said that it is sumptuously furnished inside, and not too warm, the lights being only innumerable small ones on the outside."

The two men were silent for a moment then Johnston said:

"Perhaps we might be able to get into it unobserved and be thus carried over to the other side, or reach the palace through the tunnel."

Branasko started convulsively, and then, as he looked into the earnest eyes of the American, he said despondently:

"We have got to die, anyway; it may be well for us to think of it; but on the other side, in the Barrens, there is no more chance for escape than here. But the adventure would at least give us something to think about; let's try it."

"All right; but how can we get down there where the sun starts to rise?" asked the American, peering cautiously over the edge of the hole.

"There must be some way," answered Branasko. "Ah, see! Further to the left there are some ledges; let's see what can be done that way."

"I am with you."

The rays of the departing sun were almost gone, and the electric lights down among the machinery seemed afar off like stars reflected in deep water. With great difficulty the two men lowered themselves from one sharp ledge to another till they had gone half down to the bottom.

"It is no use," said Branasko, peering over the lowest ledge. "There are no more ledges and this one juts out so far that even if there were smaller ones beneath we could not get to them."

"That is true," agreed the American, "but look, is not that a lake beneath? I think it must be, for the lights are reflected on its surface."

"You are right," answered Branasko; "and I now see a chance for us to get down safely."

"How?"

"The workers are too far from the lake to see us; we can drop into the water and swim ashore."

"Would they not hear the splashing of our bodies?"

"I think not; but first let's experiment with a big stone."

Suiting the action to the word, they secured a stone weighing about seventy-five pounds and brought it to the ledge. Carefully poising it in mid-air, they let it go. Down it went, cutting the air with a sharp whizzing sound. They listened breathlessly, but heard no sound as the rock struck the water, and the men among the machinery seemed undisturbed. Only the widening circles of rings on the lake's surface indicated where the stone had fallen.

"Good," ejaculated the Alphian; "are you equal to such a plunge? The water must be deep, and we won't be hurt at all if only we can keep our feet downward and hold our breath long enough. Our clothing will soon dry down there, for feel the warmth that comes from below."

The Alphian slowly crawled out on the sharpest projection of the ledge. "Are you willing to try it?" he asked, over his shoulder.

"Yes."

"Well, wait till you see me swim ashore, and then follow."

Johnston shuddered as the strong fellow swung himself over the ledge and hung downward.

"Adieu," said Branasko, and he let go. Down he fell, as straight as an arrow, into the shadows below. For an instant Johnston heard the fluttering of the fellow's clothing as he fell through the darkness, and then there was no sound except the low whirr of the cables and the monotonous hum of the great wheels beneath. Then the smooth surface of the lake was broken in a white foaming spot, and, later, he saw something small and dark slowly swimming shoreward. It was Branasko, and the men to the right had not heard or seen him.

Johnston saw him reach the shore, then he crawled out to the point of the projecting rock and tremblingly lowered himself till he hung downward as Branasko had done. He had just drawn a deep breath preparatory to letting go his hold, when, chancing to look down, he saw a long narrow barge slowly emerging from the cliff directly under him. For an instant he was so much startled that he almost lost his grip on the rock. He tried to climb back on the ledge, but his strength was gone. He felt that he could not hold out till the boat had passed. Death was before him, and a horrible one. The boat seemed to crawl. Everything was a blur before his eyes. His fingers began to relax, and with a low cry he fell.

Chapter X

To Thorndyke the dark corridor seemed endless. The king's last words had now a sinister meaning, and Bernardino's whispered warning filled him with dread. "Keep your presence of mind," she urged; was it then, some frightful mental ordeal he was about to pass through?

Presently they came to a door. Thorndyke heard his guide feeling for the bolt and key-hole. The rattling of the keys sounded like a ghostly threat in the empty corridors. The air was as damp as a fog, and the stones were cold and slimy. After a moment the guard succeeded in unlocking the door and roughly pushed the Englishman forward. The door closed with a little puff, and Thorndyke felt about him for the guide; but he was alone. For a moment there was no sound. With the closing of the door it seemed to him that he was cut off from every living creature. In the awful silence he could hear his own heart beating like a drum.

"Stand where you are!" came in a hissing whisper from the darkness nearby, and then the invisible whisperer moved away, making a weird sound as he slid his hand along a wall, till it died away in the distance.

A cold thrill ran over him. He was a brave man and feared no living man or beast, but the superstitious fears of his childhood now came upon him with redoubled force. For several minutes he did not stir; presently he put out his hand to the door and his blood ran cold.

There was no knob, latch, or key-hole, and he could feel the soft padding into which the door closed to keep out sound. Then he remembered the warning of the princess, and strove with all his might to fight down his apprehensions. "For your life keep your presence of mind," he repeated over and over, but try as he would his terror over-powered him. He laughed out loud, but in the dreadful silence and darkness his laugh sounded unearthly.

A cold perspiration broke out on him. It seemed as if hours passed before he again heard the sliding noise on the wall. Someone was coming to him. The sound grew louder and nearer, till a firm hand was laid on his arm; it felt as cold as ice through his clothing.

"Come," a voice whispered, and the Englishman was led forward. Presently another door opened--a door that closed after them without any sound. Here the silence was more intensified, the darkness thicker as if compressed like air.

Hands were placed on the shoulders of Thorndyke and he was gently forced into a chair. As soon as he was seated two metal clamps grasped like a vise his arms between the elbows and the shoulders, and two more fastened round his ankles.

There was a faint puff of air from the door and the prisoner felt that he was alone. Terror held him in bondage. He tried to think of Bernardino, but in vain. Did they intend to drive him to madness? He began to suspect that the king had discovered his natural superstition and had decided to put it to a test. What he had undergone so far he felt was but the introduction to greater terrors in store for him.

There was a sigh far away in the darkness--then a groan that seemed to flit about in space, as if seeking to escape the dark, and then died away in a low moan of despair. Before him the blackness seemed to hang like a dark curtain about ten yards in front of him, and in it shone a tiny speck of light no larger than the head of a pin, and which was so bright that he could not look at it steadily. It increased to the size of a pea, and then he discovered that, at times, it would seem miles away in space and then again to draw quite near to hand. Glancing down, he noticed that it cast a bright round spot about an inch in diameter on the floor, and that the spot was slowly revolving in a circle so small that its motion was hardly observable. Surely the mind of a superstitious man was never so punished! When Thorndyke looked steadily at the spot, the black floor seemed to recede, and the spot to sink far down into the empty darkness below like a solitary star; So realistic was this that the Englishman could not keep from fancying that this chair was poised in some way over fathomless space. Presently he noticed that the spot had ceased its circular movement and was slowly--almost as slowly as the movement of the hand of a clock--advancing in a straight line toward him.

No such terror had ever before possessed the stout heart of the Englishman. As the uncanny spot, ever growing brighter, advanced toward him, he thought his heart had stopped beating; his brain was in a whirl. After a long while the spot reached his feet and began

104

to climb up his legs. With a shudder and a smothered cry, he tried to draw his feet away, but they were too firmly manacled.

"It is searching for my heart," thought Thorndyke. "My God, when it reaches it, I shall die!" As the strange spot, gleaming like a burning diamond in whose heart leaped a thousand different colored flames, and which seemed possessed of some strange hellish purpose, crossed his thighs and began to climb up his body, the brain of the prisoner seemed on fire. He tried to close his eyes, but, horror of horrors! His eyelids were paralyzed. It was almost over his heart, and Thorndyke was fainting through sheer mental exhaustion when it stopped, began to descend slowly, and, then, with a rapid, wavering motion, it fell to the floor, flashed about in the darkness, and vanished.

An hour dragged slowly by. What would happen next? The Englishman felt that his frightful ordeal was not over. To his surprise the darkness began to lighten till he could see dimly the outlines of the chamber. It was bare save for the chair he occupied against a wall, and a couch on the opposite side of the room. The couch held something which looked like a human body covered with a white cloth. He could see where the sheet rounded over the head and rose sharply at the feet.

Something told him that it was a corpse and a new terror possessed him. For several minutes he gazed at the couch in dreadful suspense, then his heart stopped pulsing as the figure on the couch began to move. Slowly the sheet fell from the head and the figure sat up stiffly. There was a faint hum of hidden machinery at the couch, and a flashing blue and green line running from the couch to the wall betrayed the presence of an electric wire.

Slowly the figure rose, and with creaking, rattling joints stood erect. Pale lights shone in the orbits of the eyes and the sound of harsh automatic breathing came from the mouth and nostrils. Slowly and haltingly the figure advanced toward Thorndyke. The poor fellow tried to wrench himself free from the chair, but he could not stir an inch. On came the figure, its long arms swinging mechanically, and its feet slurring over the stone pavement.

When within ten feet of the Englishman it stopped, nodded its head three or four times, and slowly opened its mouth. There was a sharp, whirring noise, such as comes from a phonograph, and a voice spoke:

"My voice shall sound on earth for a million years after my spirit has left my body; and I shall wander about my dark dungeon as a warning to men not to do as I have done."

The voice ceased, but the whirring sound in the creature's breast went on. The figure shambled nearer to Thorndyke and the voice began again:

"I disobeyed the laws of great Alpha and her imperial king and am to die. Beware of the temptation to search into the royal motives or attempt to escape. The fate of all the inhabitants of Alpha, the wonderful Land of the

Changing Sun, is in the hands of its ruler. Beware! My death-torture is to be lingering and horrible. I sink into deepest dejection. I was eager to return to my native land and tried to escape. Behold my punishment! Even my bones and flesh will not be allowed to rest or decay. Beware, the king is just and good, but he will be obeyed!"

Slowly the figure retreated toward the couch and lay down on it. The whirring sound ceased, the light along the wire went out, and the darkness thickened till the couch and the outlines of the chamber were obscured. Then Thorndyke's chair was lifted, as if by unseen hands, and he was borne backward. In a moment he felt the cool, damp air of the corridor, and someone raised him to his feet and led him back to the throne-room.

In the bright light which burst on him as the door opened, the beautiful women and handsome men moving about the throne were to him like a glimpse of Paradise. The attendant left him at the door and he walked in, so dazed and weak that he hardly knew what to do. No one seemed to notice him and the king was engaged in an animated conversation with several ladies who were sitting at his feet.

In a bevy of women Thorndyke noticed Bernardino. She gave him a quick, sympathetic glance of recognition and then looked down discreetly. Presently she left the others and moved on till she had disappeared behind a great carved wine-cistern which stood on the backs of four crouching golden leopards in a retired part of the room. Something in her sudden movement made the

Englishman think she wanted to speak to him, and he went to her. He was not mistaken, for she smiled as he approached.

"I am glad," she whispered, touching his arm impulsively, and then quickly removing her hand as if afraid of detection.

"Glad of what?" he asked.

"Glad that you stood that--that torture so well; several men have died in that chair and some went mad."

"I remembered your advice; that saved me."

"I have a plan for us to try to rescue your friend."

"Ah, I had forgotten him! What is it?"

"Captain Tradmos likes you and has consented to aid us. We shall need an air-ship and he has one at his disposal which is used only for governmental purposes."

"What do you want with the air-ship?"

"To go beyond and over the great wall."

"But can we get away from here without being seen?"

"Under ordinary circumstances, neither by day nor night, but tomorrow the king has planned to let his people witness a 'War of the Elements.'"

"A War of the Elements?"

"Yes, the grandest fete of Alpha. There will be a frightful storm in the sky; no light for hours; the thunder will be musical and the lightning will seem to set the world on fire. That will be our chance. When it is darkest we shall try to get away unseen. We may fail. Such a daring thing has never been attempted by any one. If we are detected we shall suffer death as the penalty, the king could never pardon such a bold violation of law."

Chapter XI

Johnston clung tenaciously to the rock. He tried to look down to see if the barge had passed beneath him, but the intense strain on his arm now drew his head back, so that he could not do so. Once more he made an effort to regain his position on the rock, but he was not able to raise himself an inch.

He felt certain that the fall would kill him, and he groaned in agony. His fingers were benumbed and beginning to slip. Then he fell. The air whizzed in his ears. He tried to keep his feet downward, but it was no use. He was whirled heels overhead many times, and his senses were leaving him when he was restored by a plunge into the cold water.

Down he sank. It seemed to him that he never would lose his momentum and that he would strangle before he could rise to the surface. Finally, however, he came up more dead than alive. He had narrowly missed the flat-boat, for he saw it receding from him only a few yards away. On the shore stood Branasko motioning to him; and, slowly, for his strength was almost gone, Johnston swam toward him.

The latter waded out into the shallow water and drew him ashore.

"You had a narrow escape," he said, with a dry laugh. "I saw the boat come from under the cliff just as you hung down from the ledge. At first I hoped that you would get back on the rock, but when I saw you try and do it and fail I thought that you were lost."

The American could not speak for exhaustion; but, as he looked at the departing craft with concern, Branasko laughed again: "Oh, you thought it had a crew; so did I at first, but it has no one aboard. It is drawn by a cable, and seems to be laden with coal."

"Did they notice our fall up there?" panted Johnston, nodding toward the lights in the distance.

"No, they are farther away than I thought."

"Well, what ought we to do?" "Hide here among the rocks till our clothing dries and then look about us. We have nearly twenty-four hours to wait for the sun to return through the tunnel."

"Where is the tunnel?"

"Over on the other side of that black hill. There, you can see the mouth of the tunnel through which the sun comes."

"We need sleep," said the Alphian, when their clothing was dry, "and it may be a long time before we get a chance to get it. Let us lie down in the shadow of that rock and rest."

Johnston consented, and, lying down together, they soon dropped asleep. They slept soundly.

Johnston was the first to awake. He felt so refreshed that he knew he must have been unconscious several hours. He touched Branasko and the latter sat up and rubbed his eyes and looked about him bewildered.

"I had a horrible dream," he said shuddering. "I thought that we were in the sun and over the capital city when it fell down. I thought the fall was awful, and that all Alpha was aflame. Then the fires went out. Everything was black, and the whole world rang with cries of terrified people. Ugh! I don't want to dream so again; I'd rather not sleep at all. But hush! What is that?"

Far away, as if in the center of the earth, they heard a low monotonous rumbling. They listened breathlessly. Every moment the sound increased. They could feel the ground trembling as if shaken by an earthquake.

"It is the coming sun," said Branasko. "We must get nearer the tunnel and see what can be done. It would be useless to try to go back now."

Stealing along in the shadow of the cliffs to keep from being seen by the workmen on the plateau above, they climbed over a rocky incline and saw in the side of a towering cliff, a great black hole. It was the mouth of the tunnel. Into it ran eight wide tracks of railway and six mammoth cables each twenty or thirty feet in diameter.

"The sun cannot be far away now," remarked the Alphian.

"Is it not lighted?"

"I presume not; I think it comes through in darkness. The light is saved for its passage over Alpha."

"Would it not be as safe for us to attempt to walk through the tunnel to the palace of the king?"

"Never; it would be over fifty miles in utter darkness. There may be a thousand trestles and bridges over frightful chasms: for the most part, I have heard the tunnel is a natural channel or a succession of caverns united by tunnels. The other is the safer way, though it certainly is risky enough."

Louder and nearer grew the rumbling noise, and a faint light began to shine from the tunnel and flash on the cliff opposite.

"It is the sun's headlight," explained Branasko.

Johnston was thrilled to the center of his being as he saw the light playing over the polished tracks and cables and illuminating the walls of the great tunnel.

Suddenly there was a deep, mellow-toned stroke of a bell in the sun, and, as the two men shrank involuntarily into the deeper shade of the cliff, the great globe, a stupendous ball of crystal, five hundred feet in height, slowly emerged from the mouth of the tunnel and came to a stop under the opening in the rock which led to the space above.

"What had we better do now?" said Johnston.

"Wait," cautioned Branasko, and he drew the American to a great boulder nearer the sun, from behind which they could, without being seen, watch the action of the crowd of workmen that was hurriedly approaching. They placed ladders of steel against the sides of the sun and swarmed over it like bees.

"They are cleaning the glass and adjusting the lights," said the Alphian; "wait till they go round to the other side. Don't you see that square opening near the ground?"

The American nodded.

"It is the door," said Branasko, "and we must try to enter it while they are on the other side. Let us slip nearer; there is another rock ahead that we can hide behind." Suiting the action to the word, Branasko led the way, stooping near to the ground until both were safely ensconced behind the boulder in question. They were now so near that they could hear the electricians rubbing the glass.

One who seemed to be superintending the work opened the door and went into the sun and lighted a bright light. From where they were crouched Johnston and Branasko caught a view of a little hall, a flight of stairs, and some pictures on the walls.

Presently the man extinguished the light and came out.

"They are removing their ladders from this side," said Branasko in a whisper. "Be ready; we must act quickly and without a particle of sound. Run straight for that door and climb up the steps immediately."

The men had all gone round to the other side, and no one was in sight.

"Quick! Follow me," and bending low to the earth the Alphian darted across the intervening space and into the doorway. Johnston was quite as successful. As he entered the door he saw Branasko crawling up the carpeted stairs ahead of him, and, on his all-fours, he followed. The first landing was large, and there in the wall they found a closet. It would have been dark but for a dim light that streamed down from above. Branasko opened the closet door. "We must hide here for the present," he whispered.

They had barely got seated on the floor and closed the door when a bright light broke round them and they heard somebody ascending the stairs. The person passed by and went on further up. The two adventurers dared not exchange a word. They could hear the footsteps above and the sound of the electricians outside as they polished the lights and moved their ladders from place to place.

"If he should stay, what could we do?" asked Johnston, after a long pause, and when the footsteps sounded farther away.

"There are two of us and one of him," grimly replied the brawny Alphian.

Johnston shuddered. "Let's not commit murder in any emergency," he said.

"It would not be murder; every man has a right to save his own life."

Nothing more was said just then, for the footsteps were growing nearer. The man was descending. He crossed the landing they were on and went down the last flight of stairs and out of the door.

Branasko rubbed his rough hands together. "We are going alone," he said with satisfaction.

There was a sound of sliding ladders on the walls outside. The workmen had finished their task. A moment later a great bell overhead rang mellowly; the colossal sphere trembled and rocked and then rose and swung easily forward like the car of a balloon.

"We are rising," said the Alphian, in a tone of superstitious awe. Johnston said nothing. There was a cool, sinking sensation in his stomach and his head was swimming. Branasko, however, was in possession of all his faculties.

"We shall soon be through the shaft we first discovered and throw our light over Alpha." As he spoke the space about them broke into blinding brightness and for a few moments they could only open their eyes for an instant at a time. After a while Branasko opened the closet door and they went up the stairs.

The first apartment they entered was most luxuriously furnished. Sofas, couches and reclining-chairs were scattered here and there over the elegant carpet, and statues of gold and marble stood in alcoves and niches and strange stereopticon lanterns, hanging from the ceiling threw ever-changing and life-like pictures on the walls. The light streamed in from without through small circular windows. After they had walked about the room for some minutes, the Alphian pointed to a half-open door and a staircase at one side of the room.

"I think it leads to some sort of observatory on top," he said. "I have heard that when the royal family makes this voyage they are fond of looking out from it. Suppose we see." Johnston acquiesced, and Branasko opened the door. From the increased brightness that came in they were assured that the stairs led outward.

Ascending many flights of stairs and traversing a narrow winding gallery which seemed to be gradually sloping upward, they finally reached the outside, and found themselves on a platform about forty feet square surrounded by iron balustrades. Above hung impenetrable blackness, below curved a majestic sphere of white light.

Chapter XII

The sunlight was fading into gray when the princess turned to leave Thorndyke. Night was drawing near.

"Have they assigned you a chamber yet?" she paused to ask.

"No."

"Then they have overlooked it; I shall remind the king."

Her beautiful, lithe form was clearly outlined against the red glow of the massive swinging lamp as she moved gracefully away, and Thorndyke's heart bounded with admiration and hope as he thought of her growing regard for him. He resumed his seat among the flowers, listening, as if in a delightful dream, to the seductive music from bands in different parts of the palace and the never-ceasing sound in the air which seemed to him to be the concentrated echo of all the sounds in the strange country rebounding from the vast cavern roof.

It grew darker. The gray outside had changed to purple. In the palace the brilliant electric lights in prismatic globes refused to allow the day to die. He was thinking of returning to the throne-room when a page in silken attire approached from the direction of the king's quarters.

"To your chambers, master," he announced, bowing respectfully.

Thorndyke arose and followed him to an elevator nearby. They ascended to the highest balcony of the great rotunda. Here they alighted and turned to the right, the page leading the way, a key in his hand. Presently the page stopped at a door and unlocked it and preceded the Englishman into the room. As they entered an electric light in a chandelier flashed up automatically.

It was a sumptuous apartment, and adjoining it were several connecting rooms all elegantly furnished. The page crossed the room and opened a door to a little stairway.

"It leads to the roof," he said. "The princess told me to call your attention to it, that you might go out and view the starlight."

When the page had retired, Thorndyke, feeling lonely, ascended the stairs to the roof. It was perfectly flat save for the great dome which stood in the center and the numerous pinnacles and cupolas on every hand, and was very spacious. The Englishman's loneliness increased, for no matter in what direction he looked; there was not a living soul in sight. Far in front of him he saw a stone parapet. He went to this and looked down on the city. The electric lights were vari-colored, and arranged so that when seen from a distance or from a great height they assumed artistic designs that were beautiful to behold.

The regular streets and rows of buildings stretched away till the light in the farthest distance seemed an ocean of blending colors. Overhead the vault was black, and only here and there shone a star; but as he looked upward they began to flash into being, and so rapidly that the sky seemed a vast battlefield of electricity.

"Wonderful! Wonderful!" he ejaculated enthusiastically, when the black dome was filled with twinkling stars. He leaned for a long time against the parapet, listening to the music from the streets below, and watching the flying-machines with their vari-colored lights rise from the little parks at the intersection of the streets and dart away over the roofs like big fireflies. Then he began to feel sleepy, and, going back to his chambers, he retired.

When he awoke the next morning, the rosy glow of the sun was shining in at his windows. On rising he was surprised to find a delectable breakfast spread on a table in his sitting-room.

"Treating me like a lord, anyway," he said drily. "I can't say I dislike the thing as a whole." When he had satisfied his sharp hunger he went out into a corridor and seeing an elevator he entered it and went down to the throne-room. The king was just leaving his throne, but seeing Thorndyke he turned to him with a smile.

"How did you sleep?" he asked.

"Well, indeed," replied Thorndyke, with a low bow.

"I cannot talk to you now. I intended to, but I have promised my people a 'War of the Elements' to-day and am busy. You will enjoy it, I trust."

"I am sure of it, your Majesty."

"Well, be about the palace, for it is a good point from which to view the display."

With these words he turned away and the Englishman, as if drawn there by the memory of his last conversation with Bernardino, sought the retreat where he had bidden her good-night. He sat down on the seat they had occupied, and gave himself over to delightful reveries about her beauty and loveliness of nature. Looking up suddenly he saw a pair of white hands part the palm leaves in front of him and the subject of his thoughts emerged into view.

She wore a regal gown and beautiful silken head-dress set with fine gems, and gave him a warm glance of friendly greeting.

"I half hoped to find you here," she said, blushing modestly under his ardent gaze; "that is, I knew you would not know where to go----" She paused, her face suffused with blushes.

"I did not hope to find you here," he said, coming to her aid gallantly, "but it was a delight to sit here where I last saw you."

She blushed even deeper, and a pleased look flashed into her eyes. "It was important that I should see you this morning," she continued, with a womanly desire to disguise her own feeling. "I wanted to tell you where to meet me when the storm begins."

121

"Where?" he asked.

"On the roof of the palace, near the stairs leading down to your chambers. At first it will be very dark, and it is then that we must get out of sight of the palace. No other flying-machines will be in the air, and Captain Tradmos thinks, if we are very careful, we can get away safely before the display of lightning."

"If we find my friend what can we do with him?"

She hesitated a moment, a look of perplexity on her face, then she said: "We can bring him back and keep him hidden in your chambers till some better arrangement can be made. We shall think of some expedient before long, but at present he must be saved from starvation."

Thorndyke attempted to draw her to a seat beside him, but she held back. "No," she said resolutely, "it would never do for us to be seen together. If my father should suspect anything now, all hope would be lost."

Thorndyke reluctantly released her hand.

"You are right, I beg your pardon," he said humbly. "I shall meet you promptly. Of course I want to save poor Johnston, but the delight of being with you again, even for a moment, so intoxicates me that I forget even my duty to him."

After she left him he wandered out in the streets along the busy thoroughfares, and into the beautiful parks, the flowers and foliage changing color as each new hour dawned. The fragrance of the flowers delighted his sense of smell, and the luscious fruits hung from vine and tree in great abundance.

He was impatient for the time to arrive at which he was to meet the princess. After a while he noticed the people closing the shops and booths, and in holiday dress going to the parks and public squares. He hastened to the palace. The great rotunda and the throne-room were energetically astir. Everybody wore rich apparel and was talking of the coming fete. The king was on his throne surrounded by his men of science. In a cluster of ladies in court dress, the Englishman recognized Bernardino. Catching his eye, she looked startled for an instant, and, then, with a furtive glance at the king, she swept her eyes back to Thorndyke and raised them significantly toward his chambers. He understood, and his quick movement was his reply. He turned immediately to an elevator that was going up, and entered it. Again he was alone on the palace roof. The color of the sunlight looked so natural that he studied it closely to see if he could not detect something artificial in its appearance, but in vain. He found that it did not pain his eyes to look at the sun steadily. He took from his pocket a small sunglass, and focused the rays on his hand, but the heat was not intensified sufficiently to burn him.

Just then he heard a loud blast of a trumpet in a tall tower to the left of the palace. It seemed a momentous signal. The jostling crowds in the streets below suddenly stood motionless. Every eye was raised to the sky. Not a sound broke the stillness. Following the glances of the crowd a few minutes later, Thorndyke noticed a dark cloud rising in the west, and spreading along the horizon. A feeling of awe came over him as it gradually increased in volume, and, in vast black billows, began to roll up toward the sun.

Suddenly out of the stillness came a faraway rumble like a fusillade of cannon, now dying down low, again reaching such a height that it pained the ears. Belated flying-machines darted across the sky here and there, like storm-frightened birds, but they soon settled to earth. Every eye was on the cloud which was now gashed with dazzling, vivid, electric flashes. Thorndyke looked over the vast roof. He was alone. He walked to the western parapet to get a broader view.

The clouds had increased till almost a third of the heavens were obscured by the madly whirling blackness. There was a rumble in the cloud, or beyond it, like thunder, and yet it was not, unless thunder can be attuned, for the sound was like the music of a great orchestra magnified a thousand-fold. The grand harmony died down. There was a blinding flash of electricity in the clouds, and the Englishman involuntarily covered his eyes with his hands. When he looked again the blackness was covering the sun. For a moment its disk showed blood-red through the fringe of the cloud and then disappeared. Total darkness fell on everything.

The silence was profound. The very air seemed stagnant.

Then the wind overhead, by some unseen force, was lashed into fury, and all the sky was filled with whirlpools of deeper blackness. Suddenly there was a flash of soft golden light; this was followed by streams of pink, of blue and of purple till the whole heavens were hung with banners, flags, and rain-bows of flame. Again darkness fell, and it seemed all the deeper after the gorgeous scene which had preceded it. Thorndyke strained his sight to detect something moving below, but nothing could be seen, and no sound came up from the motionless crowds.

Behind him he heard a soft footstep on the stone tiling. It drew nearer. A hand was being carefully slid along the parapet. The hand reached him and touched his arm.

It was the princess. "Ah, I have at last found you," she whispered, "I saw you in the lightning, but lost you again."

He put his arm round her and drew her into his embrace. He tried to speak, but uttered only an inarticulate sound.

"I could not possibly come earlier," she apologized, nestling against him so closely that he could feel the quick and excited beating of her heart. "My father kept me with him till only a moment ago. Captain Tradmos will be here soon."

"When do we start?" he asked.

"That is the trouble," she replied. "We had counted on getting away in the darkness, before the display of lightning, but there is more danger now. If our flying-machine were noticed the search-lights would be turned on us and we would be discovered at once."

"But even if we get safely away in the darkness when could we return?"

"Oh, that would be easy," she replied. "As soon as the fete is over, commerce will be resumed and the air will be filled with air-ships that have been delayed in their regular business, and, in the disguises which I have for us both, we could come back without rousing suspicion. We could alight in Winter Park and return home later."

"What is Winter Park?"

"You have not seen it? You must do so; it is one of the wonders of Alpha. It is a vast park enclosed with high walls and covered with a roof of glass. Inside the snow falls, and we have sleighing and coasting and lakes of ice for skating. It was an invention of the king. The snowstorms there are beautiful."

Thorndyke's reply was drowned in a harmonious explosion like that of tuned cannon; this was followed by the chimes of great bells which seemed to swing back and forth miles overhead.

"Listen!" whispered Bernardino, "father calls it 'musical thunder,' and he declares that it is produced in no other country but this."

"It is not; he is right." And the heart of the Englishman was stirred by deep emotion. He had never dreamed that anything could so completely chain his fancy and elevate his imagination as what he heard. The musical clangor died down. The strange harmony grew more entrancing as it softened. Then the whole eastern sky began to flush with rosy, shimmering light.

"My father calls this the 'Ideal Dawn of Day,'" whispered Bernardino. "See the faint golden halo near the horizon; that is where the sun is supposed to be."

"How is it done?" asked the Englishman.

"Few of our people know. It is a secret held only by the king and half a dozen scientists. The whole thing, however, is operated by two men in a room in the dome of the palace. The musician is a young German who was becoming the wonder of the musical world when father induced him to come to us. I have met him. He says he has been thoroughly happy here. He lives on music. He showed me the instrument he used to play, a little thing he called a violin, and its tones could not reach beyond the limits of a small room. He laughs at it now and says the instrument that father gave him to play on has strings drawn from the center of the earth to the stars of heaven."

The rose-light had spread over the horizon and climbed almost to the zenith, and with the dying booming and gentle clangor it began to fade till all was dark again.

"Captain Tradmos ought to be here now," continued the princess, glancing uneasily toward the stairway. "We may not have so good an opportunity as this."

Ten minutes went by.

"Surely, something has gone wrong," whispered Bernardino. "I have never seen the darkness last so long as this; besides, can't you hear the muttering of the people?"

Thorndyke acknowledged that he did. He was about to add something else, but was prevented by a loud blast from the trumpet in the tower.

Bernardino shrank from him and fell to trembling.

"What is the matter?" he asked. "The trumpet!" she gasped, "something awful has happened!"

A moment of profound silence, then the murmuring of the crowd rose sullenly like the moaning of a rising storm; a search-light flashed up in the gloom and swept its uncertain stream from point to point, but it died out. Another and another shone for an instant in different parts of the city, but they all failed.

"Something awful has happened," repeated Bernardino, as if to herself; "the lights will not burn!"

"Had we not better go down?" asked Thorndyke anxiously, excited by her unusual perturbation.

For answer she mutely drew him to the eastern parapet. Far away in the east there still lingered a faint hint of pink, but all over the whole landscape darkness rested.

"See!" she exclaimed, pointing upward, "the clouds are thinning over the sun, and yet there is no light. What can be the matter?"

At that juncture they heard soft steps on the roof and a voice calling:

"Bernardino! Princess Bernardino!"

"It is Tradmos," she exclaimed gladly, then she called out softly:

"Tradmos! Tradmos!"

"Here!" the voice said, and a figure loomed up before them. It was the captain. He was panting violently, as if he had been running.

"What is it?" she asked, clasping his arm.

"The sun has gone out," he announced.

A groan escaped her lips and she swayed into Thorndyke's arms.

"The clouds are thinning over the sun, yet there is no light. The king is excited; he fears a panic!"

"Has such a thing never happened?" asked Thorndyke.

"An hundred years ago; then thousands lost their lives. As soon as the people suspect the cause of the delay they will go mad with fear."

"What can we do?" asked the princess, recovering her self-possession.

"Nothing, wait!" replied Tradmos. "This is as safe a place as you could find. Perhaps the trouble may be averted. Look!"

The disk of the veiled sun was aglow with a faintly trembling light; but it went out. The silence was profound. The populace seemed unable to grasp the situation, but when the light had flickered over the black face of the sun once more and again expired, a sullen murmur rose and grew as it passed from lip to lip.

It became a threatening roar, broken by an occasional cry of pain and a dismal groan of terror. There was a crash as if a mountain had been burst by explosives.

"The swinging bridge has been thrown down!" said Tradmos.

Light after light flashed up in different parts of the city, but they were so small and so far apart that they seemed to add to the darkness rather than to lessen it.

"The moon, it will rise!" cried the princess.

"It cannot," said Tradmos in his beard, "at least not for several hours."

"They will kill my father," she said despondently, "they always hold him responsible for any accident."

"They cannot reach him," consoled Tradmos. "He is safe for the present at least."

"Is it possible to make the repairs needed?"

"I don't know. When the accident happened long ago the sun was just rising."

"Has it stopped?"

"I think not; it has simply gone out; the electric connection has, in some way, been cut off."

The tumult seemed to have extended to the very limits of the city, and was constantly increasing. The smashing of timber and the falling of heavy stones were heard nearby.

Tradmos leaned far over the parapet. "They are coming toward us!" he said; "they intend to destroy the palace; we must try to get down, but we shall meet danger even there."

Chapter XIII

Johnston and Branasko looked down at the great ball of light below them in silent wonder. Johnston was the first to speak. He pointed to the four massive cables which supported the sun at each corner of the platform and extended upward till they were enveloped in the darkness.

"They hold us up," he said, "where do they go to?"

"To the big trucks which run on the tracks near the roof of the cavern; the endless cables are up there, too, but we cannot see them with this glare about us."

"We can see nothing of Alpha from here," remarked Johnston disappointedly, "we can see nothing beyond our circle of light."

"I should like to look down from this height at night," said the Alphian. "It would be a great view."

"What is this?" Johnston went to one side of the platform and laid his hand on the spokes of a polished metal wheel shaped like the pilot-wheel of a steamboat. Branasko hastened to him.

"Don't touch it," he warned. "It looks as if it were to turn the electric connection off and on. If the sun should go out, the consequences would be awful. The people of Alpha would go mad with fear."

The American withdrew his hand, and he and Branasko walked back to the center of the platform. Johnston uttered an exclamation of surprise. "The light is changing."

And it was, for it was gradually fading into a purple that was delightfully soothing to the eye after the painful brightness of a moment before.

"I understand," said the Alphian, "we are running very slow and are only now about to approach the great wall, for purple is the color of the first morning hour."

"But how is the light changed?" asked Johnston curiously.

"By some shifting of glasses through which the rays shine, I presume," returned the Alphian; "but the mechanism seems to be concealed in the walls of the globe."

Not a word was spoken for an hour. They had lain down on the platform near the iron railing which encompassed it, and Branasko was dozing intermittently. Again the light began to change gradually. This time it was gray. Johnston put out his hand to touch Branasko, but the Alphian was awake. He sat up and nodded smiling. "Wait till the next hour," he said; "it will be rose-color; that is the most beautiful."

Slowly the hours dragged by till the yellow light showed that it was the sixth hour. Branasko had been exploring the vast interior below and came back to Johnston who was asleep on the floor of the platform.

"I have just thought of something," said Branasko. "This is the day appointed by the king to entertain his subjects with a grand display of the elements."

"I do not understand," said Johnston.

"The king," explained the Alphian, "darkens the sun with clouds so that all Alpha is blacker than night, and then he produces great storms in the sky, and lightning and musical thunder. We may, perhaps, hear the music, but we cannot witness the storm and electric display on account of the light about us. It usually begins at this hour; so be silent and listen."

After a few minutes there was a rumble from below like the roar of a volcano and an answering echo from the black dome overhead. This died away and was succeeded by a crash of musical thunder that thrilled Johnston's being to its very core. Branasko's face was aglow with enthusiasm.

"Grand, glorious!" he exclaimed, "but if only you could see the lightning and the dawn in the east you would remember it all your life. The sunlight is cut off from Alpha by the clouds, and there is no light except the wonderful effects in the sky."

Johnston had gone back to the wheel and was examining it curiously.

"I have a mind to turn off the current for a moment anyway," he said doggedly; "if the sun is hidden they would not discover it."

Branasko came to him, a weird look of interest in his eyes. "That is true," he said; "besides, what matters it? We may not live to see another day."

Johnston acted on a sudden impulse. He intended only to frighten Branasko by moving the wheel slightly, and he had turned it barely an eighth of an inch, when, as if controlled by some powerful spring, it whirled round at a great rate, making a loud rattling noise. To their dismay the light went out.

"My God! What have I done?" gasped the American in alarm.

"Settled our fate, I have no doubt," muttered the Alphian from the darkness.

Johnston had recoiled from the whirling wheel, and now cautiously groped back to it, and attempted to turn it. It would not move.

"It has caught some way," he groaned under his breath.

"And we have no light to find the cause of the trouble," added the Alphian, who had knelt down and was feeling about the wheel. Presently he rose.

"I give it up," he sighed, "I cannot understand it. The machinery is somewhere inside."

"It has grown colder," shuddered Johnston.

"We were warmed by the light, of course," remarked Branasko, "and now we feel the dampness more. We are going at a frightful speed."

Just then there was a jar, and the sun swung so violently from side to side that the two men were prostrated on the floor. The speed seemed to slacken.

"I wonder if we are going to stop," groaned the American, and he sat up and held to Branasko. "Perhaps they will draw us back to rectify the mistake, and then---_"

"It cannot be done," interrupted the Alphian. "The machinery runs only one way. We shall simply have to finish our journey in darkness."

"They may catch us on the other side before the sun starts back through the tunnel," suggested the American.

"Not unlikely," returned Branasko. "There, we are going ahead again. One thing in our favor is that we can more easily escape capture in darkness than if the sun were shining."

"Does the sun stop before entering the tunnel?"

"I do not know," replied Branasko; "perhaps somebody will be there to see what is wrong with the light. We must have our wits about us when we land."

Johnston was looking over the edge of the platform. "If the king's display is taking place down there I can see no sign of it."

"How stupid of us!" exclaimed Branasko. "Of course, clouds sufficiently dense to hide the sun from Alpha would also prevent us from seeing the display below. I ought to----"

He was interrupted by a grand outburst of harmony. The whole earth seemed to vibrate with sublime melody. "Our blunder has not been discovered yet," finished Branasko, after a pause, "else the fete down below would have been over. I am cold; shall we go inside?"

Johnston's answer was taken out of his mouth by a loud rattling beneath the floor, near the wheel he had just turned; the sun shook spasmodically for an instant, and its entire surface was faintly illuminated, but the light failed signally.

"It must have been an extra current of electricity sent to relight the lamps," remarked Johnston; and, as he concluded, the sun trembled again, and another flash and failure occurred. "Look," cried the American, "the clouds are thinning; see the lights below! They have discovered the accident!"

They both leaned over the railing and looked below. As far as the eye could reach, within the arc of their vision, they could see fitful lights flashing up, here and there, and going out again. And then they heard faint sounds

137

of crashing masonry and the condensed roar of human voices, which seemed to come from above rather than from below. The Alphian turned. "I cannot stand the cold," he said.

Johnston followed him. The rapid motion of the swinging sphere made him dizzy, and he caught Branasko's arm to keep from falling.

"How can we tell when we go over the wall?" he asked anxiously.

"We shall have to guess at it," was the answer. "At any rate we must be near the lower door so as to get out quickly if it is necessary to do so to escape detection."

In the darkness they slowly made their way down the stairs to the great room.

"There ought to be some way of making a light," said the Alphian, and his voice sounded loud and hollow in the empty chamber. After several failures to find the stairs they descended to the door they had entered. Branasko opened it a little, and a breeze came in. They sat down on the stone, and after a while, in sheer fatigue, they fell asleep. Hours passed. Branasko rose with a start, and shook Johnston.

"Our speed is lessening," he exclaimed. "We must be going down. Be ready to jump out the instant we stop. There, let me open the door wider."

Chapter XIV

When Tradmos spoke the words of warning, Thorndyke put his arm round the princess and drew her after Tradmos, who was hastening away in the gloom.

"Wait," she said, drawing back. "Let us not get excited. We are really as safe here as there; for in their madness they will kill one another and trample them under foot." She led him to a parapet overlooking the great court below. "Hear them," she said, in pity, "listen to their blows and cries. That was a woman's voice, and some man must have struck her."

"Tell me what is best to do," said the Englishman. "I want to protect you, but I am helpless; I don't know which way to turn."

"Wait," she said simply, and the Englishman thought she drew closer to him, as if touched by his words.

There was a crash of timbers--a massive door had fallen--a scrambling of feet on the stone pavement, and they could see the dark human mass surging into the court through the corridors leading from the streets.

"What are they doing?" asked Thorn dyke.

She shrank from the parapet as if she had been struck.

"Tearing the pillars down," she replied aghast; "this part of the palace will fall. Oh, what can be done!"

There was a grinding of stone upon stone, a mad yell from an hundred throats, the crash of glass, and, with a thunderous sound, a colossal pillar fell to the earth. The roof beneath the feet of the princess and Thorndyke trembled and sagged, and the tiling split and showered about them.

Raising Bernardino in his arms, as if she was an infant, Thorndyke sprang toward the stairway leading to his chambers, but the roof had sunken till it was steep and slippery. One instant he was toppling over backward, the next, by a mighty effort, he had recovered his equilibrium, and finally managed to reach a safer place. As he hurried on another pillar went down. The roof sagged lower, and an avalanche of mortar and tiling slid into the court below. Yells, groans, and cries of fury rent the air.

Bernardino had fainted. Thorndyke tried to restore her to consciousness, but dared not put her from him for an instant. On he ran, and presently reached a flight of stairs which he thought led to his chambers. He descended them, and was hastening along a narrow corridor on the floor beneath when Bernardino opened her eyes. She asked to be released from his arms. He put her down, but supported her along the corridor.

"We have lost our way," he said, as he discovered that the corridor, instead of leading to his chambers, turned off obliquely in another direction.

"Let's go on anyway," she suggested; "it may lead us out. I have never been here before. I--" A great crash drowned her words. The floor quivered and swayed, but it did not fall. On they ran through the darkness, till Thorndyke felt a heavy curtain before. He paused abruptly, not knowing what to do. Bernardino felt of its texture, perplexed for an instant.

"Draw it aside, it seems to hang across the corridor," she said. He obeyed her, and only a few yards further on they saw another curtain with bars of light above and below it. They drew this aside, and found themselves on the threshold of a most beautiful apartment.

In the mosaic floor were pictures cut in colored stones, and the ceiling was a silken canopy as filmy and as delicately blue as the sky on a summer's night. The floor was strewn with richly embroidered pillows, couches, rugs and ottomans; and here and there were palm trees and beds of flowers and grottoes. A solitary light, representing the moon, showed through the silken canopy in whose folds little lights sparkled like far-off stars.

Thorndyke looked at the princess inquiringly. She was bewildered.

"I have no idea where we are," she murmured. "I am sure I have never been here before; but there is another apartment beyond. Listen! I hear cries."

"Someone in distress," he answered, and he drew her across the room and through a door into another room more beautiful than the one they had just left. Here, huddled together at a window overlooking the court, were six or eight beautiful young women. They were staring out into the darkness, and moaning and muttering low cries of despair.

"It is my father's ladies," exclaimed the princess aghast. "He would be angry if he knew we had come here. No one but himself enters these apartments."

Just then one of the women turned a lovely and despairing face toward them, and came forward and knelt at the feet of Bernardino.

"Oh, save us, Princess," she cried.

"Be calm," said the princess, touching the white brow of the woman. "The danger may soon pass; this portion of the palace is too strongly built for them to injure it." Then she turned to Thorndyke: "We must hasten on and find our way down; it would never do for us to be seen here." Then she turned to the kneeling woman and said gently: "I hope you will say nothing to the king of this; we lost our way in trying to get down from the roof."

"I will not," gladly promised the woman, and seeing that Bernardino knew not which way to turn, she guided them to a door opening into a dimly-lighted corridor. "It will take you out to the balconies and down to the audience-chamber," she said. The princess thanked her, and she and the Englishman descended several flights of stairs. Reaching one of the balconies they met the denser darkness of the outside and the deafening clang and clamor of the multitude. There was no light of any kind, and Thorndyke and his charge had to press close against the balustrade of the balcony to keep from being crushed by the mad torrent of humanity.

Now and then a strident voice would rise above the din:--

"Down with the palace! Death to the king!"

The trumpet in the tower sounded again and again.

"It is my father trying to attract their attention," explained the princess. "Something very serious has happened for once. In speaking of the time the sun went out before, he told me that he had made an invention which, in such a crisis, would instantly restore confidence to the people. I cannot understand why he does not use it. Oh, I am afraid they will kill him!"

Thorndyke tried to console her, for he saw that she was weeping, but just then there was a strange lull in the general tumult. What could have happened?

"The dawn! The ideal dawn!" cried Bernardino, pointing to the eastern sky. Thorndyke looked in wonder. A purple light had spread along the horizon, and as it gradually softened into gray and slowly turned to pink, the noise of the populace died down. No sound could now be heard save the low groans of wounded men and women. What a sight met the view as the rose-light shimmered over the city! The dead and dying lay under the feet of the crowd. Almost every creature bore some mark of violence. Eyes were blood-shot, clothing torn, limbs were bleeding, and mingled fury and sudden hope struggled in each ashen face. The young trees and shrubbery had been trampled underfoot, and walls, arcades and triumphal arches had been thrown down. The fragments of statues lay here and there, and the bodies of human beings filled the basins of broken fountains.

"It is not the sun," explained Bernardino; "but the invention my father spoke of. He is doing it to calm them."

Thorndyke made no answer. He stood as if transfixed, gazing at the horizon. The rose-light had spread over a third of the sky when gradually there appeared in its center a bright circle of yellow light. The yellow light faded, leaving a perfect picture of the throne of the king; and as the now silent masses looked at the picture, a curtain behind the throne parted and the king himself appeared. He advanced and sat on the throne, and turned a calm face towards his subjects.

"Wonderful!" ejaculated Bernardino, and her face was full of hope. "See what he will do!"

"Where is the picture?" asked Thorndyke; "can it be seen by all of—of the people?"

"Yes, by all Alpha, for it is on the sky."

Thorndyke said nothing further, for the king had stood up, and with hands out-stretched was bowing. Above the circle of light, as if cut out of the solid blackness, in flaming letters stood the word,

"SILENCE!"

And there was silence. Even the lips of the wounded men closed as the king began to speak. The sound of his voice seemed as far away as the stars, and to permeate all space:--

"All danger is over. Tidings from the west state that the sun is setting. No harm has come to it. It will rise in the morning, and the moon and stars will be out in a few hours. Let the dead be removed, the wounded cared for, and everything be repaired. This is my will."

That was all. The king bowed sedately and retired from the throne, and the circle and pink glow faded from the black sky. The stillness was unbroken for a moment, then glad murmurings were heard in all directions.

"They are lighting the palace," cried the princess. "See, down there is the arcade leading to the rotunda."

"I am glad it is over," said Thorndyke.

She grasped his arm and impulsively looked into his face. "But your friend, we have forgotten him, and done nothing to save him, and now it is too late."

"We could not help it; we had to think of our own safety."

"I shall send for Captain Tradmos and try to devise some other plan," she said, as they descended the stairs.

"We should not be seen together," she added, as they approached the throne-room; "besides, you ought to go to your chambers. No one is allowed to be out when the dead is being removed."

"Where is the dead taken?"

"Over the wall, to be burned in the internal fires," she concluded, as she was leaving him.

He found everything in order in his rooms and he lay down and tried to sleep, but he was too much excited over the happenings of the day. Hours must have passed when his attention was drawn to a bright light shining on the wall of his room. He went to a window and looked out on the court. The light came from the rising moon.

Below lay the ruins of fallen columns, capitals, cornices and statues. Figures in black cloaks and cowls were removing the dead from the debris. With a fluttering sound something swooped down past his window to the ground. It looked like a great bird, carrying the car of a flying-machine. Thorndyke watched its circular descent to the earth, and shuddered with horror as the black figures filled the car with bodies and the gruesome machine spread its wings and rose slowly till it was clear of the domes and pinnacles of the palace, and then flew away westward.

Other machines came, and, one after another, received their ghastly burdens and departed. In a short time all the dead was removed, and hundreds of workmen came from the palace and began repairing the fallen masonry.

Thorndyke went back to his couch and tried to sleep, but in vain. Slowly the hours of night passed, and as the purple of dawn rose in the east he dressed himself and went up on the roof. The moon had gone down and the stars were fading from the sky. The dark earth below showed no signs of life; but as the purple light softened into gray he saw that the streets of the city were filled with silent expectant people, all watching the eastern sky. And, as the gray light flushed into rose, and the rose began to scintillate with gold, they began to stir, and a hum of joyful voices was heard. The promised day had come.

Chapter XV

The sun was, indeed, slowing up. The two men peered out at the door.

"It would be unlucky for us if it should not come so near to the earth as it did on the other side," whispered Branasko.

"I can hardly feel any motion to the thing at all," replied the American. "Look! For some reason it is not so dark below. I can see the rocks. Surely we have already passed over the wall."

"That's so," returned the Alphian. "Come; we must be quick and watch our opportunity to land. I can't imagine where the light comes from unless it is from the people waiting for the arrival of the sun." Every instant the speed was lessening. Overhead the cables were beginning to creak and groan, and, now and then, the great globe swung perilously near some tall stony peak, or passed under a mighty stalactite. Slower and slower it got till, when within a few feet of the ground, it stopped its onward motion and only swung back and forth like a pendulum.

"Quick," whispered Branasko, "we must get down while it is swinging, no time to lose--not an instant!" And as the sun moved backward, with his hand on the doorsill, he leaped to the earth. Johnston followed him.

They were not a moment too soon, for about fifty yards away they saw a body of sixty or seventy men with lights in their hands hastening toward them.

"Just in time," exulted Branasko, and he quickly drew Johnston into a little cave in the face of a cliff. Crouching behind a great rock, they saw and heard the men as they approached.

Some of them walked around the sun, and two, evidently in authority, entered the door. The others were placing ladders against the side of the sphere, when suddenly there was a loud clattering in the interior, a whirling of wheels under the platform above, and the surface of the sun burst into light.

The two refugees were momentarily blinded. Branasko had the presence of mind to quickly draw his companion down close to the earth behind the rock. "They could see us in the light," he whispered.

There was a joyous clamoring of voices among the men, and they withdrew several yards to look at the sun. This drew them nearer the hiding-place of the two refugees.

"Only an accident," said a voice; "it won't happen again."

Then one of them went into the sun and the lights died out. In a moment the sun began to move. Slowly and majestically it swept over the rocky earth, followed by the crowd, till it reached a great hole and sank into it.

"Gone into the tunnel," said the Alphian, as the crowd disappeared behind the cliff.

"What are we to do now?" asked Johnston. "We certainly can't go through with the sun."

"Wait till the next trip," grimly replied Branasko.

The rumbling noise from the big hole gradually died away, and the two men left their hiding-place.

"What is that?" asked Johnston. He pointed to the west, where a red light shone against the towering cliffs.

"It must be the internal fires," answered Branasko, with a noticeable shudder. "Let's go nearer; I have heard that there is a point near here where one can look down into the Lake of Flame."

"The Lake of Flame!" echoed the American, "What is that?" "It is where all of the dead of Alpha is cast by the black 'vultures of death.'"

Johnston said nothing, for it was difficult to keep up with the Alphian, who was bounding over rocks and dangerous fissures toward the red glowing the distance.

At every step the atmosphere got warmer, and they detected a slight gaseous odor in the air. Finally, after an arduous tramp of an hour, they climbed up a steep hill and looked sharply down into a vast bubbling lake of molten matter more than a thousand yards below. Branasko noticed a stone weighing several tons evenly balanced on the verge of the great gulf, and pushed it with both his hands. It rocked, broke loose from its slender hold on the cliff and bounded out into the red space. Down it went; lessening as it sank till it became a mere black speck and then disappeared.

"That's where the dead go," said Branasko gloomily.

Just then the American, happening to glance up, saw something like a huge black bird with outspread wings circling about in the red light over the pit. Branasko saw it, too, and his face paled and a tremolo was in his voice when he spoke.

"It is one of the 'vultures of death;' don't stir; we won't be seen if we remain where we are!" The strange machine sank lower over the lake of fire, till, as if buoyed up on the hot air, with faintly quivering wings, it paused. A man opened a door of the black car and carelessly threw out the bodies of a woman and a child.

The bodies whirled over and over and disappeared in the pit, and the man closed the door. The machine then rose and gracefully winged its flight to the east. In a moment others came with their grim burdens, and still others, till the mouth of the pit was dark with them.

"Something has happened," whispered Branasko, "some great calamity, for surely so many people do not die in Alpha in a single day."

For an hour they watched the coming and going of the vultures, till, finally the last one hovered over the lake of fire. Suddenly the machine swerved so near to Branasko and Johnston that they shrank close to the earth to keep from being seen. Something was evidently wrong with the machine, for there was a wild look of desperation on the driver's face as he tugged excitedly at the pilot-wheel. But all his efforts only caused the air-ship to dart irregularly from side to side, and, now and then, to strike the rocks of the pit's mouth, to shoot up suddenly, or to sink dangerously down toward the fire.

"He is losing control of it," whispered Branasko, "he does not know what to do. See, he is trying to lighten the load, by kicking out the body."

That was true, and, as the machine made a sudden plunge toward the cliff a few yards to the left of the refugees, the dead body, which the driver had managed to move to the door with his feet, fell out and lodged upon the edge of the cliff instead of falling into the fiery depths. The machine bounded up a few yards and paused, now apparently under the control of its driver. The man looked down hesitatingly at the corpse for a moment and then lowered the machine to the sloping rock near where the body lay. He alighted and cautiously crept down the steep incline to the body. He raised it in his arms and was about to cast it from him when his foot slipped, and with a cry of horror he fell with his burden over the cliff's edge into the red abyss.

Johnston uttered an exclamation of horror, but Branasko was unmoved. After a moment he rose, and carefully scanning the space overhead, he crawled on hands and knees toward the machine. Johnston heard him chuckling to himself and uttering spasmodic laughs, and he watched him closely as he reached the machine. For several minutes he seemed to be inspecting it critically, both inside and out; then he stood away from it, a bold, black silhouette on a background of flame, and motioned the American to come to him.

Johnston promptly, but not without many misgivings, obeyed his signal. "What are you up to?" asked he, as the Alphian assisted him to rise from his hands and knees.

Branasko touched the machine and smiled. His face was shining with enthusiasm.

"The question of our returning to Alpha is settled," he said sententiously.

"How?"

"We can go in this."

"Can you manage it?"

"Easily; that fellow must have been drunk; the machine is in good order, I think."

"When do you propose to start?" and the American eyed the funeral-car dubiously.

"The night is before us; we could not get a better time." As he spoke he entered the car and laid his hand on the wheel. Johnston, obeying his nod, followed, shuddering as he remarked the traces of blood on the floor.

"All right!" Branasko turned the wheel slowly, and the wings outside began to flap, and the car mounted into the air like a startled bird and flew out quickly over the pit.

Branasko bit his lip, and Johnston heard him stifle an exclamation of impatience. As for the American, he was at once thrilled and fascinated by the awful sight below; he could now see beneath the overhanging mouth of the pit, and look far down into a boundless lake of molten matter that seemed as restless as an ocean in a storm.

Then the air became so hot he could hardly breathe. He looked at the Alphian in alarm. The latter was whirling the wheel first one way and then another with a startled look of fear in his eyes, and then Johnston noticed that the walls of the pit were rising about them, and the black canopy overhead rapidly receding.

They were sinking down into the fire.

Almost wild with terror, the American sprang toward the wheel, but Branasko pushed him away roughly.

"Stand back," he ordered gruffly. "It is the heat; let me alone!"

The American sank into his seat. The heat became more and more intense. Both men were purple in the face, and the perspiration was rolling from their bodies in streams. Down sank the machine.

"I can't manage it," said Branasko hoarsely, "we'd as well give up." Just then Johnston noticed the mouth of a cave behind Branasko.

"Look," he cried, "can't we get into it?"

Branasko looked over his shoulder, and, as he saw the cave, he uttered a glad cry. He quickly turned the wheel and drew out a lever at his right. The machine obeyed instantly; it swerved round suddenly and dived into the cave. The cool air soon revived them, and Branasko had little trouble in bringing the car to a resting-place on the rocky floor of the cave. Before them hung impenetrable darkness, behind a curtain of red light.

"We are in a pretty pickle now," said Johnston despondently, as they alighted from the car.

"Nothing to do but to make the best of it," sighed Branasko.

"Perhaps this cave may lead out into some place of safety."

Johnston's eyes had become somewhat accustomed to the gloom, and he began to peer into the darkness.

"I see a light," he exclaimed; "it cannot be a reflection from the fire in the pit, for it is whiter."

The Alphian gazed at it steadily for a moment, then he said decidedly: "We must go and see what it is." Without another word he started toward the white, star-like spot, sliding his hand over the rocky wall, and springing over a fissure in the floor.

Gradually the light grew brighter, till, as they suddenly rounded a cliff, a grand sight burst upon their view. They found themselves in a vast dome-shaped cavern, thousands of yards in diameter and height. And almost in the center of the floor, from a red and purple mound of cooling lava, leapt a white stream of molten matter from the floor to the dome. And in the black dome, where the lava turned to molten spray, hung countless stalactites of every color known to the artistic eye. And from the foot of the fountain ran a tortuous rivulet that lighted the walls and roof of a narrow chamber that extended for miles down toward the bowels of the earth.

Branasko was delighted.

"The king does not know of this," he declared, "else he would make it accessible to his people, and call it one of the wonders of Alpha. By accidentally sinking into the pit we have discovered it. But," he concluded, "We must at once try to find some way out other than that by which we came."

They turned from the beautiful fountain, and, holding to each other's hands, and aided by the light behind them, they stumbled laboriously through the semi-darkness. Branasko's ears were very acute. He paused to listen.

"Hark ye!" he cautioned.

The combined roar of the pit and the fountain of lava had sunk to a low murmur, but ahead of them they now heard a rushing sound like a distant tornado.

"Come on," said the Alphian, and he drew his companion after him with an eagerness the American was slow to understand. The light in the cavern gradually grew brighter. By a circuitous route they were again approaching the pit of fire, though it was still hidden from sight.

Finally they reached a point where the wind was blowing stiffly, and further on a volume of cold spray suddenly dashed upon them and wet them to the skin. And when their eyes had become accustomed to the rolling mist, they saw a great lake, and pouring into it from high above was a mighty waterfall.

"Mercy!" ejaculated the Alphian, in great alarm. "If this is salt water we are lost. All Alpha will come to an end!"

"What do you mean?" And Johnston wondered if Branasko's trials and struggle could have turned his brain.

"If it be salt water, then it has broken in from the ocean above Alpha," he explained. "The king has often said

157

that not a drop of the ocean has ever entered the great cavern."

Branasko stooped and wet his hand in a little pool at his feet. "I am almost afraid to taste it," said he, holding his hand near his mouth. "It would settle all our fates." He waited a moment and then touched his fingers to his tongue.

"Salt!" That was all he said for several moments. He folded his arms and looked mutely toward the boiling lake. Presently he raised his eyes to the great hole in the roof, and groaned: "The break is gradually widening. These stones are freshly broken, and the great bowl is filling."

"It will fill all Alpha with water and drown every soul in it," added the terrified American.

"That, however, is not the most immediate danger," said Branasko wisely. "They would first suffocate, and later their bodies would be swallowed up in the stomach of the earth."

"What do you mean?"

Branasko shrugged his shoulders. "As soon as this bowl is filled with water, which would not take many hours, it would run over into the lake of fire and produce an explosion that would rend Alpha from end to end."

"Who knows, it might turn the whole Atlantic into the center of the earth, and destroy the entire earth." But

Branasko was unable to grasp the full magnitude of the remark, for to him the world was simply a vast cavern lighted by human ingenuity. He fastened a narrow splinter of stone upright in the shallow water at his feet, and, lying down on his stomach with his eyes close to it, he studied it for several minutes. When he got up, a desperate gleam was in his dark eyes.

"It is rising fast," he said. "We must attempt to get to the capitol and warn the king. It is possible that he may be able to stop the opening. The only thing left to us is to try our machine again."

Johnston found it hard to keep pace with him as he bounded out of the mist and on toward the faint glow ahead. Reaching the flying machine Branasko entered it and turned on a small electric light.

"Ah," he grunted with satisfaction, "I have found a light. I can now see what is the matter with it."

Johnston stood outside and heard him hammering on the metal parts in the car, and became so absorbed in thinking of the peril of their position that he was startled when Branasko cried out to him:--"All right. I think we can make it do; a pin has lost out, but perhaps I can hold the piece in place with my foot. If only we can stand the heat of the pit long enough to rise above it, we may escape."

Johnston followed him into the car. Branasko seated himself firmly and gave the wheel a little turn. Slowly the machine rose. "See!" cried Branasko, "it is under control. We must not be too hasty. Now for the pit!"

The heart of the American was in his mouth as the long black wings waved up and down and the air-ship, like some live thing, shuddered and swept gracefully out of the mouth of the cave into the glare and heat of the pit.

"Hold your breath!" yelled Branasko, and he bent lower into the car to escape the shower of hot ashes that was falling about them. Far out over the lake in a straight line they glided, and there came to a sudden halt. Johnston's eyes were glued on his companion's face. Branasko sat doubled up, every muscle drawn, his eyes bulging from their sockets. Would he be strong enough? To Johnston everything seemed in a whirl. The walls of the pit were rising around them.

Chapter XVI

Thorndyke went down into his chambers to make his toilet and was ready to leave when there was a soft rap on his door. He opened it, and to his surprise saw Bernardino modestly draw herself back into the shadow of the hall.

"Pardon me, but I must speak to you," she stammered in confusion.

"What is it?" he asked, going out to her.

"I want to advise you to avoid my father to-day. He is greatly disappointed with the accident of yesterday, and he is never courteous to strangers when he is displeased. He was particularly anxious to have you entertained by the fete."

"Thank you; I shall keep out of his way," promised the Englishman. "Where had I better stay--here in my rooms?"

"No, he might send for you. If you would care to see Winter Park, I can go with you as your guide."

"I should be delighted; nothing could please me more."

"But," (as a servant passed in the room with a tray) "that is your breakfast. Meet me at the fountain at the north entrance of the palace in half an hour." And, drawing her veil over her face, she vanished in the darkness of the corridor.

After he had breakfasted and sent the man away, he hastened below to the place designated by the princess. She was waiting for him under the palm trees, and was so disguised that he would not have known her but for her low amused laugh as he was about to pass her.

"It would not do for anyone to suspect me," she explained; "my father would never forgive me for doing this." She pointed to a flying-machine nearby. "We must take the air; I have made all the arrangements. Winter Park is beyond the limits of the city."

He followed her across the grass to the machine and into the car. They could see the driver behind the glass of the narrow compartment in which he sat, and when he turned the polished metal wheel the machine rose like a liberated balloon.

Thorndyke looked out of the window. The blue haze of the fifth hour of the morning was breaking over everything, and as the domes, pinnacles, and vari-colored roofs fell away in the beautiful light, the breast of the Englishman heaved with delightful emotions. Bernardino was watching his face with a gratified smile.

"You like Alpha," she said, half anxiously, half inquiringly.

"Very much," he replied; "but I want to show you the great world I came from;--and someday perhaps I can."

The blood ran into her cheeks suddenly, and then as quickly receded, leaving a wistful expression in her eyes. She sighed. "It has been my dream for a long time. I have always imagined that it is more wonderful than Alpha; but you know there is no chance for you to return now."

"I shall manage to escape some way and you shall go with me as my wife."

Her blushes came again. "I did not know that you cared that much for me," she said. Then, as if to change the subject, she pointed through the window. "See, we are approaching the Park, and shall descend in a moment."

He looked out of the window and then drew his head in quickly.

"We are coming down into a big lake!" he cried out. "Oh, no, it is only the glass roof of the park," she laughed; "true, it does look like water in the sunlight."

The machine sank lower and finally rested on a plot of grass in a little square ornamented with beds of flowers and white statues. Thorndyke saw a seemingly endless wall, so high that he could not calculate its height. Bernardino preceded him in at a great arching door in the wall, and they found themselves in a stone-paved vestibule several hundred feet square.

A maid servant came forward at once and brought heavy fur clothing for them and invited them into separate toilet rooms. When he came out Bernardino was waiting for him. He could hardly breathe, so thick were the furs he had put on.

"It is warm here, but it will be colder in a moment," said the princess. And she led him to a door across the room. When the door was opened, Thorndyke uttered an exclamation of astonishment. Before their eyes lay a wide expanse of snow-covered roads, woodlands, and frozen lakes and streams. The air was as crisp and invigorating as a Canadian winter.

Bernardino led him to a pavilion where a number of pleasure-seekers were gathered and selected a sleigh and two mettlesome horses. She took the reins from the man, and sprang lightly into the graceful cutter. Thorndyke followed her and wrapped the thick robes about her feet. Away they sped like the wind down the smooth road, through a leafless forest. Overhead the glass roof could not be seen, but a lowering gray cloud hung over them and a light snow was falling.

"Winter Park is a great resort," the princess explained; "we get tired of the unchanging climate, and it is pleasant to visit such a place as this. There is a winter park in every town of any size in Alpha."

They drove along the shore of a beautiful lake, on the frozen surface of which hundreds of skaters were darting here and there, and passed hillsides on which crowds of young people were coasting in sleds. When they had driven about ten miles in a circuitous route she turned the horses round.

"We had better return," she said; "you have not seen all of the Park, but we can visit it some other time."

Outside they found their flying-machine awaiting them, and were soon on the way back to the city. They parted at the fountain in the park, she hastening to the palace, and he turning to stroll through the little wood behind him.

He was passing a thick bunch of trees when he was startled by hearing his name called. He turned round, but at first saw no one.

"Thorndyke!" There it was again, and then he saw a hand beckoning to him from a hedge of ferns at his right. He stepped back a few paces; a man came out of the wood.

It was Johnston; his face was white and haggard, his clothing rent and soiled.

"My God, can it be you?" gasped the Englishman.

"Nobody else," groaned Johnston, cautiously advancing and laying a trembling hand on the arm of Thorndyke; "but don't talk loud, they will find me."

"Where did you come from?"

Johnston pointed first to the east, and then swept his hand over the sky to the west.

165

"Over the wall," he said despondently. "From the dead lands behind the sun."

"How did you get back here?"

For reply Johnston parted the fern leaves and pointed to the lank figure of the tall Alphian, who lay curled up on the grass as if asleep. "He brought me in that flying-machine there; but he has spent all his strength in trying to manage the thing, which was out of order, and now he is helpless. Twice we came within an inch of sinking down into the internal fires. The last time we escaped only by the breadth of a hair; if he had not had the endurance of a man of iron he would have succumbed to the heat and we would have been lost. We sank so far down that I became insensible and never knew a thing till the fresh air revived me. See, my beard and hair are singed, and look how he is blistered. Poor fellow! He is a hero." Johnston stepped back and shook the Alphian, but the poor fellow's head only rolled to one side, showing his bloodshot eyes. He was insensible.

"He is in a bad fix," said Thorndyke; "where did he come from?"

"Banished like myself; we met over there in the dark and roamed about together."

"What are you going to do?"

"I don't know; I was following his lead. We will both be put to death if we are discovered."

"Did he not tell you his plan?"

Johnston started visibly. "Oh, I forgot," he exclaimed. "He declares that all this vast cavern is in danger. Over in the west we discovered a hole in the roof through which the ocean is streaming in a torrent. He calculated that before many hours the water would overflow into the internal fires and produce a volcanic eruption that will swallow up all of Alpha."

"Merciful Heaven! And you are hiding here at such a moment? The king must be informed at once."

Johnston had grown suddenly paler. "It may not be as bad as Branasko feared, and the king would have no mercy on me and him."

"Leave that to me," said Thorndyke; "I have made a good friend of the Princess Bernardino. She will tell me what is best to do. Remain here."

In breathless haste, Thorndyke went into the audience chamber. Fortunately the king was not on his throne, and he caught sight of the confidential maid of the princess.

She saw him approaching, and withdrew behind a cluster of tall white jars of porcelain containing rare plants.

"I must see your mistress," he said; "tell her to come to me at once; we are in great peril!"

The girl swept her eyes over the balconies and the throne and said: "She is in her apartments, sir; I shall bring her."

"Tell her to meet me at the fountain where we last met," and he hastened back to the spot mentioned.

She soon came. "What is it?" she asked excitedly.

"Johnston is back," he replied. "He is in the wood there with a fellow who escaped with him in a disabled flying-machine. He says the sea has broken through over in the west and is streaming into Alpha in a torrent."

"Surely there is some mistake," she said; "such a thing has never happened."

"It may have been caused by the explosives during the storm," went on Thorndyke. "Branasko, the Alphian who was with Johnston, says we are in imminent peril."

"There must be some mistake," she repeated incredulously, as she looked to westward. The green glow of the second hour of the afternoon lay over everything. She stood mute and motionless for a long time, looking steadily at the horizon; then she started suddenly, changed her position, and shaded her eyes from the sunlight.

"It really does seem to me that there is a cloud rising, and it is unlike any cloud I ever saw."

"I see it too!" cried the Englishman; "it must be that the water has already reached the internal fires."

Bernardino was very pale when she turned to him.

"My father must know this at once; come with me."

Into the palace, through the vast rotunda, past the throne, and into the very apartment of the king himself she led him hastily. A royal attendant met them and held up his hands warningly. "The king is asleep," he said in an undertone.

"Wake him--wake him at once!" commanded the excited girl.

"I cannot, it would offend him," was the reply.

She did not pause an instant, but darting past the man and running to the king's couch, she drew the curtain aside and touched the sleeper. He waked in anger, but her first word disarmed him.

"Alpha is in danger."

"What!" he growled, half awake. "The sea is breaking through in the west, and running into the internal fires."

"How do you know that?"

"A dense cloud is rising in the west, and:----"

169

"Impossible!" the word came from far down in his throat, and he was ghastly pale. He ran to the table and touched a button and, to the astonishment of Thorndyke, the walls on the western side of the room silently parted, showing a little balcony overlooking the street below. The king went hastily out and looked toward the west. The others followed him. The princess stifled a cry of alarm when she glanced at the sky.

Great black, rolling clouds were rapidly spreading along the horizon.

The king looked at them as helplessly as a frightened child. "The air!" he groaned. "It is hot!" and then he held out his hand to the princess, and showed her a flake of soot on it, and he dumbly pointed to others that were falling about them.

"How did you discover it?" he asked, and Thorndyke saw that he was trying to appear calm.

"Mr.--this gentleman's friend has returned from banishment, and----"

"Returned! Has the wall been destroyed?"

"No; he accidentally discovered the danger, and came in a flying-machine to warn you."

"Where is he? Bring him to me, quick!"

"But you will not ----"

He waved his hand impatiently. "Go; if Alpha is saved he shall be at liberty--if it is not, what does it matter?"

Thorndyke hastened away after Johnston, who, when he was told of the king's words, readily accompanied his friend to the presence of the ruler. They found him with his daughter still on the balcony.

"How did you discover this?" asked the king, turning to the American.

As quickly as possible, Johnston related his adventures, and particularly the story of the shooting fountain and the fall of salt water. The king did not wait for him to conclude. He ran back into his chamber, touched another button, and the next instant alarm-bells were ringing all over the city.

"A signal to the protectors," explained the princess to Thorndyke; "by this time they are ringing all over Alpha. Oh, what will become of us?" as she spoke she leaned over the balustrade and looked down into the street. Vast crowds had gathered and were motionless, except at points where the purple-clad "protectors" rushed from public buildings to assemble in squads on the street corner.

Chapter XVII

Bernardino turned to look after her father as he was leaving the room.

"He is going to the observatory," she said to Thorndyke and Johnston. "Let us go also." And they followed the king into the room with the glass roof and walls covered with mirrors which he had shown the strangers several days before. A white-headed old man stood at the stand, his fingers trembling over the half circle of electric buttons. In a mirror before him he was studying the reflection of a town of perhaps a hundred houses. The streets were filled with excited citizens, and a squad of protectors stood ready for action near a row of flying-machines.

"Ornethelo," said the king, and at the sound of his voice the old man turned and bowed humbly.

"All right," went on the king, "I will take your place a moment."

He went to the stand and touched a button. Instantly the scene changed; fields, forests, streams and hills ran by in a murky blur, and then a larger town flashed on the mirror. Here the same stir and alertness characterized the scene. The gaze of every inhabitant was fixed on the threatening horizon. Rapidly the scenes shifted at the king's will, till a hundred cities, towns and villages had been reviewed.

"Enough! They are all ready--all faithful," groaned the king, "and, Ornethelo, they may all have to perish to-day, and all for our ambition. Poor mortals!"

Ornethelo's face was half submerged in the beard on his breast, but he looked up suddenly and spoke:

"For their sakes, then, we ought not to delay; there may yet be hope."

"You are right, Ornethelo." There was a ring of hope in the voice of the king. "Quick! Show me my capitol, that I may see if all the protectors are ready."

Ornethelo touched another button, and, as if seen from a great height, the fair and wondrous city dawned before the eyes of the spectators. In every street policemen and protectors and flying-machines stood in orderly readiness. The housetops were colored with the variegated costumes of men, women and children. Over all lay the wondrous sunlight, through the green splendor of which the flakes of soot were falling like black snow.

The king touched the old man's arm. "I must see beyond the walls; are the connections made?"

"Ready, sir."

"Try them; they must not fail me now!"

The old man tremblingly unlocked a cabinet on the table, and another row of electric buttons was displayed.

173

Ornethelo touched one. Immediately there was a sharp clicking sound under the stand, and the view was swept from the mirror. Nothing could be seen but a dark suggestion of towering cliffs and yawning caverns.

"Not the east, Ornethelo," cried the king impatiently. "Go on! The west! The west!"

The black landscape flashed by like a glimpse of night from a flying train, and then a blur of redly illuminated smoke in rolling billows seemed to swell out from the surface of the mirror into the room.

"There, slow!" cried the king, and then a frightful scene burst upon their sight. They beheld a great belching pit of fire and flames. The sky from the earth to the zenith was a vast expanse of illuminated smoke, and the black landscape round about was cut by rivulets of molten lava rolling on and on like restless streams of quicksilver.

The king leaned against the stand as if faint with despair. "Call Prince Arthur!" he ordered, and almost at that instant the young man appeared.

"Father!"

The king pointed a quivering finger at the mirror, and said huskily:

"Let not the sun go down! Let its light be white as at noon."

"But, father, it has never been done before; it----"

"Alpha has never faced such danger. All our dream is about to end. Go!"

Without a word the young man hastened away, and it seemed scarcely a moment before the sunlight streaming in at the oval glass roof changed from green to white.

The king pushed Ornethelo impatiently aside; his eyes held a dull gleam of despair, and he seemed to have grown ten years older. He touched a button, and the awful scene at the pit gave place to a bright view of the capitol, which was plainly seen from its crowded center to its scattering suburbs. The squads of "protectors" stood like armies ready for battle, their rigid faces still toward the awful west.

"They are ready--the signal!" yelled the king, waving his hand, "the signal!" Ornethelo caught his breath suddenly and tottered as he went across the room, and touched a button on the wall. The king's eyes were glued on the mirrored view of the capitol, his trembling hands held out, as if commanding silence. Then a deafening trumpet blast broke on the ear. The masses of citizens pressed near the edges of the roofs and close against the walls along the streets, as the protectors rushed into the flying-machines. Another trumpet-blast, and away they flew, a long black line, every instant growing smaller as it receded in the murky distance. The princess, white and silent, led Thorndyke and Johnston back to the balcony. The line of machines was now a mere thread in the sky, but the ominous cloud in the west had increased, and fine sand and ashes were added to the fall of soot.

"What was that?" gasped the princess. It was a low rumble like distant thunder, and the balcony shook violently.

"An earthquake," said Thorndyke. "I am really afraid there is not a ghost of a chance for us; the water running into the fire is sure to cause an eruption of some sort, and even a slight one would be likely to enlarge the opening to the ocean."

Johnston nodded knowingly as he looked into his friend's face, but, considering the presence of the princess, he said nothing.

"My brother, Prince Marentel, is the greatest man in our kingdom," she re marked. "He has taken enough explosives to remove a mountain."

"How will he use them?" asked Thorndyke.

"I don't know, but I fancy he will try to close the opening in some way."

The latter slowly shook his head. "I fear he will fail. The fall must be as voluminous as Niagara by this time."

"My father must have lost hope, or he would not have stopped the sun," sighed the princess, and she cast a sad glance towards the west. The rolling clouds had become more dense, and the rumbling and booming in the distance was growing more frequent. A thin gray cloud passed before the sun, and a dim shadow fell over the city.

"That is a natural cloud," said Thorndyke; "it comes from the steam that rises from the pit."

"It is exactly like our rain clouds," returned the princess; "but it comes from the steam, as you say. But let us go into the Electric Auditorium and hear the news. As soon as anything is done we will hear of it there." The others had no time to question her, for she was hastening into the corridor outside. She piloted them down a flight of stairs into a large circular room beneath the surface of the ground. It was filled with seats like a modern theatre, and in the place where the stage would have been, stood a mighty mirror over a hundred feet square. She led them to a private box in front of the mirror. The room was filled from the first row of chairs to the rear with a silent, anxious crowd. In the massive frame of the mirror were numerous bell-shaped trumpets like those on the ordinary phonograph, though much larger.

"Watch the mirror," whispered Bernardino as she sat down.

And at that instant the surface of the great glass began to glow like the sky at dawn, and all the lights in the room went out. Then from the trumpets in the frame came the loud ringing of musical bells.

"They are ready," whispered Bernardino; "now watch and listen."

The pink light on the mirror faded, and a life-like reflection appeared--the reflection of a young man standing on a rock in bold relief against a dark background of rugged, slabbering cliffs and the forbidding mouths of caves.

"Waldmeer!" exclaimed the princess, and she relapsed into silence.

The young man held in his hand a cup-shaped instrument from which extended a wire to the ground. He raised it to his lips, and instantly a calm, deliberate voice came from the mirror, soft and low and yet loud, enough to reach the most remote parts of the great room.

"The ocean," began he, "is pouring into the 'Volcano of the Dead' in a gradually increasing torrent. Prince Marentel hopes temporarily to delay the crisis by partially turning the torrent away from the pit into the lowlands of the country. For that purpose a portion of the endless wall is being torn down, and Marentel's forces are placing their explosives. After this is done an attempt will be made to stop the original break. There is, however, little hope. The prince has warned the king to be prepared for the worst."

At this point, the speaker turned as if startled toward the red glare at his right. He quickly picked up another instrument attached to a wire and put it to his ear. A look of horror changed his face as he turned to the audience and began to speak:--"The opening in the wall is not progressing rapidly. Workmen are drowning and the tunnel of the sun is filling with water. It will be impossible for the sun to go through to the east."

Just then there was a far-away crash, and instantly the mirror was void. There was now no sound except the low groans of women in the audience and the subdued curses of maddened men. The silence was profound. Then the mirror began to glow, and the image of another man took Waldmeer's place.

"It is the Mayor of Telmantio," whispered the princess, "a place near the western limits of Alpha."

He held a like instrument to the one used by Waldmeer, and through it spoke:--"Venus, one of the great stars, has been shaken from the firmament. It fell in the suburbs of Telmantio, and many lives were lost."

That was all, and the figure vanished. Presently Waldmeer reappeared. He seemed to be standing nearer the pit, for entire background was aflame; volumes of black smoke now and then hid him from view, and a thick shower of ashes and small stones were falling round him. He spoke, but his voice was drowned in a deafening explosion, and the whole landscape about him seemed afire. In the semi-darkness hundreds of protectors could be seen struggling in the rushing water, moving stones and building a dam. Waldmeer again faced his far-off audience and spoke:--"Prince Marentel has turned the course of the stream. All now depends on the success or failure of his final test with explosives, which will take place in about half an hour."

"We ought to go outside again," suggested Bernardino, as Waldmeer's image disappeared; "my father might want us."

Seeing no one in the king's apartment, they passed through it to the balcony. Half the sky was now covered with mingled fog and smoke, and the sun could be seen only now and then. A drizzling rain was falling—a rain that brought down clots of ashes and soot. But this made no difference to the throngs in the now muddy and slippery streets. They stood shivering in damp and soiled clothing, their blearing eyes fixed hopelessly on the lowering signs in the west. Johnston noticed a bent figure crouched against a wall beneath them. It was Branasko.

"Who is it?" inquired the princess.

"Branasko, the companion of my adventures," he replied.

"Call him to us," she said eagerly, and the American went down to the Alphian.

As they entered together, Branasko uncovered his disheveled head and bowed most humbly.

"You look tired and sick and hungry; have you eaten anything today?" she asked.

"Not in two days," he replied.

The princess called to a frightened maid who was wringing her hands in a corridor.

"Give this man food and drink at once," she ordered, and Branasko, with a grateful bow and glance, withdrew. Johnston followed him to the door.

"Fear nothing," he said. "If the danger passes we are safe; the king has promised to pardon me, and he will do the same for you."

"There is no hope for any of us," replied Branasko grimly; "but I do not want to die with this gnawing in my stomach; adieu."

"If the worst comes, is there any chance for us to escape from here to the outer world?" the Englishman was asking the princess when Johnston turned back to them.

"For a few hundred, yes,--by the sub-water ships, but for all, no; and, then, my father would not consent to rescue a part and not the whole of his subjects. He would not try to save himself or any of his family."

The clouds still covered the sun; but on the eastern sky its rays were shining gloriously. Ever and anon there sounded from afar a low rumbling as if the earth were swelling with heat.

Johnston left the two lovers together and went to the door of the Electric Auditorium, and over the heads of

181

the breathless crowd he watched the great mirror. After a few moments Waldmeer appeared and spoke:

"Prince Marentel is operating with great difficulty. A large quantity of his explosives has been injured by water, but he hopes there is enough left intact to serve his purpose. The final explosion will soon take place. The greatest peril hangs over Alpha."

Waldmeer's reflection was becoming in-distinct, and sick at heart the American elbowed his way through the muttering crowd into the corridor. Here he met Branasko, and together they walked back to Thorndyke and the princess, who were mutely watching the signs in the east. Just then the sun slowly emerged from the cloud.

"Look!" cried Bernardino in horror. "The cloud is not moving; the sun has not stopped! It is going down and we shall soon be in utter darkness. Oh, it is awful--to die in this way!"

The king had just returned, and he over-heard her words. He came hastily to the edge of the balcony, and gazed at the sun. The others held their breath and waited. His face became more rigid; he swayed a little as he turned to her.

"You are right, my daughter," he groaned; "it is going down; the cowardly dogs in the east have deserted their posts. It is going down! It will sink into a tunnel filled with water, and the light of Alpha will be extinguished forever. We are undone! Say your prayers, my child, your prayers, I tell you, for an Infinite God is angry at our pretensions!"

"Don't despair, father," and Bernardino put her arms gently round the old man's neck. "You understand the solar machinery; could you not stop the sun?"

The eyes of the old man flashed. He seemed electrified as he drew himself from her embrace and looked anxiously over the balustrade to a flying-machine in the street below.

"I might reach the east in time," he cried; "yes, you are right, I was acting cowardly. The fastest air-ship in Alpha is ready, and Nanleon can drive it to its utmost speed. If the worst comes, I shall see you no more, good-bye!" He kissed her brow tenderly, and her eyes filled as he hastened away. Down below they saw him spring lightly into the gold-mounted car, and the next instant the graceful vessel rose above the palace roof and sped like an arrow across the sky toward the east.

A faint cheer broke from the lips of the crowd which seemed suddenly to take new hope from the king's departure. Some of them waved their hats and scarfs, and many watched the air-ship till it had disappeared in the murky distance.

"He may not get there in time!" cried the princess; "it seems to be going down faster than it ever did before, and he has a great distance to go."

The little party on the balcony were silent for a long time. Presently Bernardino turned her tearful eyes to the face of Thorndyke.

"The smoke and steam do not seem so voluminous; do you think all will go well?"

The Englishman slowly shook his head. "I don't want to depress you more than you are; but I think at such a time we ought to realize the worst. It is true, the clouds are not so heavy, and the earth-quakes are less frequent, but, unfortunately, it is owing to the fact that the volume of water has been turned away from the pit into the tunnel. Be prepared for the worst. If your father cannot reach the machinery in the east soon enough, our light will go out; and, worse than that, if Prince Marentel should fail in his next venture with explosives, all hope will be gone."

"I have never desired to live so much as now," she answered, inclining with an air of tenderness toward him. "I never knew what it was to fear death till--till you came to us."

He made no reply. There was a lump in his throat and he could not trust his voice to speech. Branasko and Johnston left them together to go into the Electric Auditorium. They returned in great haste.

"The prince is ready for the explosion," panted Johnston. "Thorndyke, old man, this is simply awful! It is not like standing up to be shot at, or being jerked through the clouds in a balloon. It seems to me that out

184

there is the endless space of infinity, and that all the material world is coming to an end. My God! Look at that hellish fire, the awful smoke and that black sky! Oh, the blasphemy of such a paltry imitation of the handiwork of the Creator! We are damned! I say damned, and by a just and angry God!"

"Don't be a fool," said Thorndyke, and he threw a warning glance at Bernardino, who, with staring, distended eyes was listening to Johnston.

"No, he is right," she said in a low tone. "I have never seen your world, but I know my people must be woefully wrong. In your land they say men teach things about Infinity and an eternal life for the soul; and that one may prepare for that life by living pure, and in striving to attain a high spiritual state. Oh, why have you not told me about that? It is the one important thing. I have long wanted to know if my soul will be safe at death, but I can learn nothing of my people. They have always tried to rival God, and, in their mad pursuit of perfection in science, they have been reduced to--this. That black cloud is the frown of God, hose mad flames may burst forth at any moment and engulf us."

She uttered a low groan and hung her head as if in prayer. Johnston and Thorndyke were awed to silence. Never had the Englishman loved her as at that moment. She was no longer simply a beautiful human creature, but a divinity, speaking truths from Heaven itself. He felt too unworthy to stand in her presence, and yet his heart was aching to comfort her.

185

She raised her pallid face heavenward and extended her fair, fragile hands toward the lowering sky and began to pray. "My Creator," she said reverently, childishly, "I have never come to Thee, but they say that people far away from this dark land, under Thy own sun, moon and stars do ask aid of Thee, and I, too, want Thy help. Forgive me and my people. They have been sinful, and vain, and thoughtless, but let them not perish in utter gloom. Forgive them, O thou Maker of all that exists-- thou Creator of pain that we may love joy, Creator of evil that we may know good, turn not from us! We are but thoughtless children—and Thy children--give us time to realize the awful error of our hollow pretensions! Give them all now, at once, if they are to die, that spirit which is awakened in me by the awful majesty of Thy anger! Hear me, O God!" And with a sob she sank on her knees, clasped her hands and raised them upward. Thorndyke tried to lift her up, but she shook her head and continued her prayer in silence. A marked change had come over Branasko. He looked at Johnston and Thorndyke in a strange, helpless way, and then, in a corner of the balcony the begrimed and tattered man fell on his knees. He knew not the meaning of prayer, but there was something in the reverent attitude of the princess that drew his untutored being toward his Maker. He covered his face with his hands and his shaggy head sank to his knees.

Johnston hastened back into the Auditorium. Returning in a moment, he found the Englishman tenderly lifting Bernardino from her knees and Branasko still crouching in a corner.

"What is the news?" asked Thorndyke.

"Everything is ready for the explosion. The prince seems only waiting because he dreads failure. The people in there are so frightened that they cannot move from their seats."

Just then Branasko raised a haggard face and looked appealingly at the princess. She caught his eye.

"Fear nothing, good man," she said; "the God of the Christians will not harm us; we are safe in His hands. I felt it here in my heart when I prayed to Him. Oh, why has my father and the other kings of Alpha not taught us that grand simple truth! But before I die I want to leave this dark pit of sin, and look out once into endless, world-filled space."

A joyous flush came into the face of the Alphian. His fear had vanished. She had promised him safety. He bowed worshipfully, but he spoke not, for Bernardino was eagerly pointing to the sun.

"Look!" she cried gleefully, with the merry tremolo of a happy, surprised child. "The sun is not moving. Father has been successful! It is a good omen! God will save us!"

It was true; the sun was standing still. A deep silence was on the city. The crowds in the street neither moved nor spoke. Without a murmur or complaint they stood facing the frowning west. Suddenly the silence was interrupted by a low volcanic rumble. The earth heaved, and rolled, and far away in the suburbs of the city the spire of a public building fell with a loud crash. A groan swept from mouth to mouth and then died away.

"The cloud is increasing rapidly," said Thorndyke. "I can really see little hope. I shall return in a moment."

While he was gone Bernardino knelt and prayed. Again overcome with fear Branasko crouched down in his corner. Another shudder and rumble from the earth, another long moan from the people. Thorndyke came back. He spoke to the princess:

"The dam built by Prince Marentel has been swept away. The ocean is pouring into the internal fires. There is scarcely any hope now."

Branasko groaned, but Bernardino's face was aglow with celestial faith. She shook her head.

"They will not be destroyed in this way," she said; "they have had no chance to know God."

"It all depends on the explosion which may take place at any moment," and Thorndyke took her into his arms and whispered into her ear, "I do not care for myself; but I cannot bear to think of your suffering pain."

She answered only by pressing his hand. The clouds were now rolling upward in greater volume than ever. It was growing darker. The little group on the balcony could now scarcely see the people below them. The fall of damp ashes was resumed. The air had grown hot and close.

Boom! Boom! Boom! The streets of the city rose and fell with the undulating motion of a swelling sea. Blacker and blacker grew the sky; closer and closer the atmosphere; damper and damper became the fog; thicker and thicker fell the wet sand and ashes.

"Perhaps we would be safer in the streets," suggested Thorndyke, drawing Bernardino closer into his arms, "the palace may fall on us."

But the princess shook her head. "Father would not know where to find me, I shall await him here." Branasko had edged nearer to her. His eyes were glued on her face and he hung on her words as if his fate were in her hands. He had no regard for the opinions of the others.

"The explosion will soon take place now unless something has happened contrary to the expectations of the prince," said the Englishman.

Boom! Boom! Kr-kr-kr-kr-boom! The noise seemed to shake the earth to its center. Now the far-away pit was belching forth fire and molten lava rather than steam and smoke. The flames had spread out against the sloping roof of the cavern, and seemed to extend for a mile along the horizon. "They can do nothing in that heat," exclaimed Johnston; "they could not get near enough to the pit. Thorndyke, old fellow, I can't see a ghost of a chance. We might as well say good-bye."

189

"Hush!" It was the voice of the princess. "I feel that we shall not be lost, I say." And as she spoke Branasko crept toward her and raised the hem of her gown to his white lips. Something dark came between them and the far-off glare. It was a flying-machine.

"It is father," cried Bernardino, and she called out to him: "Father! Father! Here we are, waiting for you!" In a moment he was with them.

"All right in the east," he said gloomily. "Baryonay is there. They deserted him, but they returned when the flames went down. This is awful, daughter; it means death! It means annihilation!"

She put her arms round his neck and drew his face close to hers. "No, no," she said earnestly; "I see with a new light--a new spiritual light. There is mercy in the divine heart of Him that made the walls of our little world and constructed countless other worlds. I have prayed for mercy, and into my heart has come a sweet peace I never knew before. We shall not be lost. He will give us time to give up our sinful life here and seek Him."

The old man quivered as with ague; he searched her face eagerly, drew her spasmodically into his arms, and then sank to the floor, overcome with exhaustion.

The roar in the west was increasing. Hot ashes, gravel and small stones were falling on the roofs and the people. Now and then a cry of pain was heard, but they would not seek the shelter of the buildings. If they had to die they wanted to fall facing the enemy. Suddenly the king rose. He looked to the west and groaned. Something told them that the explosion was coming. Expectation, horrible suspense was in the air. There was a mighty flare of light. The entire heavens were lighted from horizon to horizon, and then the light went out.

"Oh, I thought it----" but the princess did not finish her sentence.

"The explosion," said Thorndyke, "the sound will follow in a moment."

"My God, have mercy on us!" cried the king. But his prayer was drowned in a deafening sound. Bernardino had leaned into the arms of her lover. "Don't despair," he said tenderly, "the prince may have been successful."

"I feel that he has," she replied. "But, oh, it is dreadful!"

The crowds below seemed to understand that their fate depended on the news that would reach them in a few minutes.

Boom! Boom! Kr-kr-kr-kr-boom! There seemed to be no lessening of the volcanic disturbance, and the earth groaned and rocked and quivered as before.

"It is impossible to tell yet," groaned the king. "Oh, God, save us; give us a chance to escape this awful doom!"

Johnston bethought himself that he might learn something in the Electric Auditorium and he went into it. It was empty and dark; not a soul was there save himself. He was turning to leave when his eye was drawn to the great mirror by a faint pink glow appearing upon it. He stood still, a superstitious fear coming over him as he thought of being alone with a possible messenger from the far-away scene of disaster. The light went out tremblingly; then it flashed up again, and the American thought he saw the face of Waldmeer. The light grew steadier, stronger. It was Waldmeer, but he was submerged in smoke. Hark! He was speaking.

"Marentel is successful! Entrance closed temporarily, and will be strengthened!"

Johnston rushed out to the balcony. "I have been to the Auditorium," he announced. "I have seen Waldmeer. He says the experiment was successful. It is closed temporarily, and can be strengthened."

The king grasped the hand of the American. "Thank God!" he exclaimed, "if I can only save my people I shall desire nothing more." The princess moved toward him affectionately, but he put her aside and retired into the palace.

"He will at once communicate with the people," remarked Bernardino hopefully, and she turned her face again toward the west. The red glare was dying down, and the dense clouds in the sky were thinning. In an hour the face of the sun broke through the smoke, and the flying-machines of the protectors began to return.

That night the king caused the pink light of the "Ideal Dawn" to flood the eastern sky, and, as before, he appeared in a circle of dazzling light and addressed his subjects:

"All danger to life is over; but the ultimate fate of Alpha is sealed. Prince Marentel has effectually closed the entrance of the ocean, but the internal fires are gradually burning through the rocky bed of the ocean. In a couple of years Alpha will be demolished. All our wealth shall be equally distributed among you, and my ships shall transport you to whatever destination you desire. Let there be no haste. Order shall be preserved throughout."

That was all. The king bowed and the picture faded from view. A deep silence was over everything. The only light came from the stars and from the moon. Then there was a sound like the wind passing over a vast forest of dry-leaved trees--the people were returning to their homes.

"I should have thought they would greet the king's announcement with a cheer of joy," said Thorndyke to the princess, as they returned to the palace.

"They don't know whether to weep or laugh," she replied. "They love Alpha, and the other world will be strange to most of them. As for myself, now that I am to leave, I feel a few misgivings."

"I shall see that you are perfectly happy," he said tenderly. "You are to be my wife. I shall always love you and care for you; you need have no fears."

And a moment later, with joyous tears and face aglow, she assured him she had none.

THE END